B

Riley's Fire

Also by LEE MERRILL BYRD

My Sister Disappears: Stories and a Novella

RILEY'S FIRE

A NOVEL

by Lee Merrill Byrd

A SHANNON RAVENEL BOOK
Algonquin Books of Chapel Hill 2006

R

A SHANNON RAVENEL BOOK

Published by
ALGONQUIN BOOKS OF CHAPEL HILL
Post Office Box 2225
Chapel Hill, NC 27515-2225

a division of
WORKMAN PUBLISHING
708 Broadway
New York, New York 10003

Printed in the United States of America.
Published simultaneously in Canada by Thomas Allen & Son Limited.
Design by Anne Winslow.

Library of Congress Cataloging-in-Publication Data
Byrd, Lee Merrill.
Riley's fire : a novel / by Lee Merrill Byrd.—1st ed.
p. cm.
"A Shannon Ravenel book."
ISBN-13: 978-1-56512-497-4; ISBN-10: 1-56512-497-9
1. Boys—Fiction. 2. Children—Hospital care—Fiction.
3. Burns and scalds—Patients—Fiction. 4. Burns and scalds in children—Fiction. 5. Shriners Burn Institute (Galveston, Tex.)—Fiction. 6. Galveston (Tex.)—Fiction. I. Title.
PS3552.Y674R55 2006
813'.54—dc22 2005053072

10 9 8 7 6 5 4 3 2 1
First Edition

To God be the glory,

Great things He has done!

About the same time the Queen of Paflagonia presented His Majesty with a son and heir; and guns were fired, the capital illuminated, and no end of feasts ordained to celebrate the young Prince's birth. It was thought the fairy, who was asked to be his godmother, would at least have presented him with an invisible jacket, a flying horse, a Fortunatus's purse, or some other valuable token of her favour; but instead, Blackstick went up to the cradle of the child Giglio, when everybody was admiring him and complimenting his royal papa and mamma, and said, "My poor child, the best thing I can send you is a little misfortune"; and this was all she would utter.

—William Makepeace Thackeray
The Rose & The Ring

Author's Note

Riley's Fire is a work of fiction. While it is based on experience, all names, characters, and incidents are either products of my imagination or are used fictitiously. No reference to any real person is intended or should be inferred.

Some readers may know the Shriners hospital in Galveston well, so I want to note that *Riley's Fire* is set at the *original* Shriners Burns Institute, which was located at 610 Texas Avenue. It was in use until May of 1992, when the new hospital, the Shriners Hospital for Children in Galveston, opened up at 815 Market Street.

Riley's Fire

Seven-year-old Riley Martin arrived at the Shriners Burns Institute in Galveston, Texas, on the twenty-second day of February, fourteen hours after he suffered third-degree burns to sixty-three percent of his body. He and his parents were flown from El Paso in a small private jet donated by a local corporation.

1

At first he'd been alone on a high bed in a dark room. That was nearly everything he remembered except that his mother and his father were there with him.

His mother sat in a chair on one side of his bed. He could feel her even when he didn't want to open his eyes to look at her. Her voice slipped in and out of his mind the way Lady Luck scampered in and out of the side door of his house back in El Paso, scratching for attention until someone let her in.

He could feel his father, too, moving back and forth between a chair in a corner of the room and the end of Riley's bed. *Oh honey,* his father would cry out, *you're shivering so bad*. A chair would scrape against the floor. After a long while, there would be a pressure at the bottom of his bed and his father's hand would be on the cover right over one of his feet.

Your mother and I are right here, sweetheart. Stay with us. Don't go anywhere.

His father seemed to come from very far away to touch his feet, his breathing came so hard. As soon as he could, Riley meant to look over and see if the room was slanted. The chair where his father sat must be at the bottom of a hill and the hill must have been so steep, it took forever to climb.

Remember what that doctor said? he heard his mother murmur. *So much skin gone, nothing to hold the heat.*

Riley?

His mother said she was sewing—pajamas for his teddy bear—out of some material she bought at the Holiday Mall, a place behind the hospital. She was pasting all the get-well cards that people were sending into a little blue book she had also bought at the mall.

Grandma says she loves you, she said in her best reading voice.

And look at this, Lewis, she said, her voice no longer for him. *A check from your mother. Oh, so generous. We need that.* From far away, his father groaned.

She went on. *Ginny says that Sarah says hello.*

Greg misses you. He says that you are his best friend.

Mrs. Althoff has sent a picture of all the kids in your

class waving at you—and there's Greg right in front. Can you see that, dear?—she held it in front of his eyes. *See? I'll paste that on the inside front cover.*

Betsy says she is knitting you a sweater.

Oh look—Vicki drew a picture of a flying lion. Where should I put that?

More money . . .

The chair scraped. His father stood up.

Mrs. Pino says that the radio station in El Paso told everyone all about the plane that flew us here. They announced when the plane left El Paso so early the morning after the fire and then they announced when we landed in Galveston.

Do you remember the plane, Riley? Do you remember flying over the water?

Riley?

RILEY?

One morning it was still night and his mother and father were there already and he woke up and saw them standing around his bed. His father's hair was sticking out all over his head. The nurse came in. *Just a little something to relax him,* she said and he drifted back in and out of sleep and then they rolled his bed down a narrow hall—*Mommamommamomma*—into a room that was all bright lights and noises and people moving around and whispering. He was shaking, his body wouldn't quit shaking, and a man with very shiny black hair and black glasses put a bad-smelling rubber mask over his face and said, *I hear your name is Riley. Count backward now, Riley, starting at ten*, but he could only get to five before he started traveling down a long tunnel that led to his dining room rug and a sudden hope that Greg would come visit and they could lie on their backs with their knees up and listen to the tape of the Lone Ranger—*Hi Ho, Silver!*—but before ever Greg showed up at the door, a lady stood next to his ear and yelled and yelled at him to wake up, *WAKE UP, RILEY*, as if he were dead.

Oh watch out now, you're throwing up—

RILEY?

It was his father. He was sitting in the chair beside his bed where his mother usually sat. His mouth was very close to Riley's head and he was talking so quietly and so fast that Riley had to shut his eyes tight just to keep up. His father's breath was very warm.

Can you hear me, sweetheart?

Riley?

I was just thinking about that time when you were in the Christmas play. Do you remember when you were in the Christmas play?

There was a Christmas play at Memorial Park Preschool when Riley was five and Riley was picked as one of the three Wise Men and Riley's father had laughed and called the Wise Men the three wise guys. Riley couldn't find the play anywhere in his memory but his father—so tall and lean and funny, his slanty eyebrows and scratchy moustache and his hair that curled every whichway, his backward-doubling knees, the gasping laughter that always suddenly poured out of him, his cheeks turning red and the color rising right into the roots of his hair—his father joking about the wise guys and standing in the middle of their living room on a night late in December when the light was already gone by the time he got home from work—his father Riley *did* remember. His father's delight he remembered—that and the fact that he thought maybe his father shouldn't have made fun of the Wise Men, shouldn't have called them wise guys. Somehow it didn't seem right.

But the play he didn't remember.

His father went on anyway, one word tumbling over another, talking about Riley and how busy he always was, how he was always talking and talking and going around and telling his mother and father all about everything, like what he was going to wear for the play and what the teacher wanted him to do and say and how his mother was working so hard to get everything right, just the way Riley kept telling her she had to do. The teacher said he had to have a robe, so his mother had found an old red velvety bathrobe that was hanging in his father's closet, one he never wore, and she had made a sash out of one of his father's neckties and put it around Riley's waist and then she took a towel and put it over Riley's head like a desert nomad and then she tied that on with another necktie.

You were spectacular, Riley! It was all your mother's doing—she knows how to turn a bunch of neckties and an old bathrobe into a regular sheik of Arabee!

After Mary and Joseph appeared and Joseph tripped over the too-long bathrobe *his* mother made him wear, Riley came striding out with the other Wise Men following him and marched right to the very center of the stage and set his feet just so, just like he was a samurai warrior, and his robe was half falling off and his mother and father could see his dungarees that his mother had cut off below the knee so they wouldn't show beneath the robe. And then, to everyone's amazement and delight, Riley stuck his arms out toward the audience and yelled as loud as he could, *Oh, holy night!* in exactly the same way Riley's grumpy old grandmother from New Jersey always said, *Oh, holy mackerel!*—scratching her old, gray head and trying to remember where the heck she'd laid down her glasses or where she'd parked the car.

Riley's mother and father got such a kick out of that, that his mother wrote the whole story down in her diary and then sent a copy of her notes to both sets of grand-parents and to all Riley's aunts and uncles and everyone in the audience laughed and clapped so loud.

Try to remember, sweetheart. You were five years old. You were the hit of the Christmas play. Your mother wrote it all down in her diary. You watched her write it down.

Remember, Riley?

2

Riley?

Your father and I have been walking and walking whenever we're not here with you, his mother said. *Early in the morning when we walk, the air is so thick with water because of the ocean so close that you can hear it slip down the green glide-y leaves of the magnolia trees that are everywhere. It drops on the sidewalks, which are covered entirely with tiny pieces of broken seashells.*

Riley often thought of that sound—water sliding down leaves, dropping on seashells—as he listened to his mother talk. Her voice was like a rope, a long rope like the kind lifeguards throw out into the water. It was the only thing that kept him from floating away for good.

That—and his father's hand on his feet.

We walked all week. That's what they did when they weren't there with Riley in his room—because the hospital would only let them visit between eight in the morning and one in the afternoon and then three in the afternoon until seven-thirty at night. When they couldn't be with him, they walked and they talked. They talked about everything, his mother said—about what the doctor said and about what the doctor didn't say and about what the nurse said, whichever one was on the most recent shift, about the kids they'd seen racing up and down the halls in the hospital, about all the people they kept meeting, about—well, there wasn't anything they didn't talk about.

They would come to the hospital early, as soon as they were allowed. They'd come from whatever motel they were staying in.

The first two nights they were in Galveston, they had stayed at a Holiday Inn near the hospital. That was the place where they had called everyone on the phone: Grandma and Grandpa Martin in Memphis and Grandma and Grandpa Grider in New Jersey and Uncle Roddy and Uncle Doug and Aunt Peggy and all their friends who didn't live in El Paso and told them about Riley. Everything had happened too fast—the fire, the ambulance, the hospital, the doctors telling them they had to go to Galveston right away, the plane, all within fourteen hours, and there hadn't been time to let people know.

It was during those first two days—right as soon as

they arrived in Galveston—that they'd sat in a little room on the third floor of the hospital waiting and waiting for the doctors to look at Riley and tell them . . . what they could—even though the doctors in El Paso had already told them more than they could bear. Kids who were already in the hospital ran up and down the halls in front of the room where they waited, laughing and playing, the backs of their hospital gowns flying open so you could see their underpants—if they had them! But nobody seemed to care whether they did or not. They were like Peter Pan's lost boys, laughing and screaming just as if they were—as if they were—regular—

It was during those first two days that they'd met Dr. Walker, the head doctor, a tall man with an English accent and a long, thin nose and a very kind way of explaining things that made his mother cry and his father leave the room and pace the hall back and forth. While the nurses were putting Riley in the tubs and getting him settled in what they called isolation, Dr. Walker sent them down to talk to the social worker, Melinda Kepler, and they had stayed there for an hour, talking and talking. *It was nice to talk,* his mother said. *I need to talk.* Her voice shook. *Your father doesn't like to talk the way I do.* Melinda Kepler had told his mother that everything she was feeling was entirely appropriate.

Lewis? Do you think that's the sort of language social workers use?

It was during those first two days that they'd also met the dietitian—*what's her name?*—a lady who wore a white jacket like a doctor and had a pink smile and was much too cheerful for his mother. It was the dietitian who told them that Riley could only drink milk. It was because he'd lost so much skin and was therefore losing calories all the time. That meant he couldn't have sodas, not even water. No empty calories, is what the pink dietitian had said. But since he couldn't drink anything anyway, they would get all that milk into his stomach through the tube that was in his nose. And they'd get the water into him through an IV in his arm.

They'd also talked to a lady named Marilyn Hooper who was the psychiatrist at the hospital. She had been burned herself. You could tell by her arms, Riley's mother said, which were ripply. Marilyn Hooper told his mother that she and her husband and two sons were in their house in Nevada when a forest fire rose up out of nowhere and trapped them inside. She said her boys were taken to one hospital and she and her husband were in another hospital, both of them in the same room. When she and her husband finally got out of the hospital four months later, they got a divorce. *This fire will either make you or break you*, Marilyn Hooper said, and it had obviously broken her. But she was a lady his mother liked a lot—*even if that advice was strange, didn't you think, Lewis? Especially telling you right away when you first get here.*

There had also been a medical reporter from Houston who had gone into the operating room to film Riley's first surgery because Dr. Walker had alerted her that Riley's case would be an interesting one. The reporter—a slender lady in black high heels—was worn out when she finally got to talk to Riley's mother and father, who by that time—with so many people to meet and talk to and all the thinking they were doing about Riley—were very dull. The reporter's cameraman, George, was very hot and very cranky. The reporter asked if she could come interview them when Riley was getting ready to leave the hospital. *Whenever that would be.*

During those first two days, they'd also discovered the cafeteria across the street from the hospital and they would go there very early in the morning and have breakfast and wait until they were allowed to come to Riley's room. Eggs and bacon and whole wheat toast with grape jelly. The cafeteria was full of people. Some were families like them, waiting for their kids and fathers and wives and grandmothers who were sick in the hospitals that were all around—the Shriners Burns Hospital, they found out, was just one of several hospitals, all within walking distance. Others were doctors and nurses, residents and interns. There were also some men there in the cafeteria who were bankers, sitting with their legs crossed in their pinstriped suits and ties and smoking cigarettes. They didn't talk to each other. They didn't look at each other. They just talked to the air, as if everything they had to say was so important.

Dead men!—a bunch of bankers in a small town. They didn't even know about us, they didn't even know you were here in the hospital, Riley. All they could think about was themselves.

They would get to Riley's room by eight in the morning, she said, and they'd wait there for Dr. Walker to make his rounds with all his students—the Shriners hospital was a teaching hospital. Dr. Walker would tell his mother and father to go out in the hall while he looked Riley over and talked to his students about Riley's case. They would have to wait outside the door until Dr. Walker was finished and then he would come out and tell them how Riley was doing that day and if he was any—better. Or worse.

Dr. Walker says you're a very fine boy, Riley. He says he can tell.

When visiting hours were over for the morning, they would go eat lunch at a place called Rusty's and then they would walk some more. Walk and talk. Up to the beach, all along the beach—*I love the beach, you know I do, Riley*—down by the bay, all along the streets full of old houses—

One day we walked on the wharf going out into the bay, Riley. We saw lots of fishing boats. We saw a kingfisher. Your father said that's the sign of Jesus.

Where did you hear that from, Lewis?

The chair scraped against the floor, his father's hand against his feet.

Your father will need to go home at the end of the week, Riley. He has to go to work. But he'll be back. Today we need to go look for another motel. The Holiday Inn is too expensive.

Riley?

Riley?

He could feel the warmth coming from his father's breath.

Your mother is taking a break this morning, his father said. *She's going to buy herself a new blouse or something*, his father said—something nice so that she could look pretty for Riley. His father said he really liked

Galveston and he thought that Riley would like it, too. Everybody in the hospital—*well, only the black women, but they were most of the people*—called him honey. He loved being called honey. It made him feel like he was back home in Memphis, a place he only liked because the black women there called him honey, too. He said he told one of the nurses, a black man named Gene, that he noticed that here in Galveston the women called him honey, and Gene had said, Oh yes, they notice quality when they see it.

His father said he was glad to be alone with Riley for a change and that as he sat there next to Riley he'd got to thinking about Riley, about how early Riley always liked to get up in the mornings back home.

Sometimes it's five-thirty!—and I'm still asleep!

His father's voice was all broken, like it was full of water. He said he loved the way Riley was in the morning and that even though he and Riley's mother were still asleep, in their dreams they could hear Riley drag the dining room chair across the kitchen floor to the cabinet so he could get down his Wheaties. They thought his love for Wheaties was a genetic thing because Riley's Uncle Roddy and Uncle Douglas, who Riley barely knew, also loved Wheaties and also ate them sitting alone at their respective dining room tables in Pennsylvania and California early in the morning. Riley's mother and father could hear Riley pour his Wheaties into his bowl, which he got by opening another cabinet and slamming it shut. Later they could see the Wheaties all over the dining room rug and they often wondered if Riley didn't know where his mouth was, he missed it so much, or if the mess on the rug was because he was talking too much. They decided it was because he was talking so much because they could hear him as he sat at the old, round dining room table in the early morning light, chewing and slurping, talking things over with himself, busy busy busy with sorting out the business of the world. Riley was always full of spit and chatter in the gloomy dawn.

But once he finished his Wheaties and even before he took his bowl over to the sink and washed it out, Riley went into his mother and father's bedroom and climbed right back into bed with them. And when he was in bed with them, he kept right on talking, even though his mother and father were dead asleep. *Hey, Mom!* he would say, *hey, Mom. Did you know the Pilgrims made two mistakes?*

Do you remember when you asked her that, Riley?

And then Riley would poke his father with his foot and he would say, *Hey, Dad!* And if it was the weekend, he would always say, *Can I help you with anything today, Dad?*—because Riley always wanted to help.

But Riley's mother and father were both so lazy that they never answered him. They just kept right on sleeping, but that never bothered Riley for a minute. He just kept talking. He lay on his back and he peered up at the ceiling and he started having some sort of battle—lining up his soldiers, commanding his troops. Riley's battles were always between himself and Greggie's cousin Jason, that guy who was forever butting into his friendship with Greg. There in the ceiling Riley would set up sides—Riley's mother and father could hear all this happening even as they tried to catch a few more minutes of sleep before the day began—Riley and Greg against Jason, the battle laid out clean and sharp, nothing but the clearest images, with Riley at the center as the constant victor, the commander of every army.

That's you, Riley, that's you—the constant victor, the wonderful boy who talks to himself while he eats his Wheaties in the early morning light.

His father must have gone away because it was completely silent in the room, not the scrape of a chair, not a breath. Riley slept. Then later, close by his ear—*don't let yourself go away, don't let yourself forget who you are, don't let yourself forget that we love you.*

3

They ended up staying in a motel by the ocean, his mother said, a place they had found on the long walk they took one afternoon. In the afternoon, that motel had seemed like a nice motel. It was on the main street that ran along beside the Seawall. In the afternoons, people rented bikes and roller skates so they could ride and skate and mothers and fathers and children strolled along the Seawall and the ocean crashed against the shore like lions roaring and the sun, even in February, made the water jump with yellow light. In the afternoons, you could smell salt in the air and feel it sticky on your skin and see the sandpipers and hear them cheep-cheep-cheeping as they paraded on their tiny legs along the beach.

Oh, Lewis, if we could just bring Riley down to the ocean, I know he would be healed. Completely—just one dip in the ocean—we could go home—

Lewis?

RILEY?

Riley? We found your mother a room in the mother's dorm. It's right across the street. She'll be here every day just like usual and the hospital has her phone number at the mother's dorm, so anytime day or night, she can be right here. You don't need to worry.

Riley's father said that tomorrow was Sunday and that he was leaving very early in the afternoon so he could catch the plane back to El Paso. He had been in Galveston all week—ever since the day after the fire—but now he had to go back home. He had to take care of Lady Luck—the neighbors couldn't keep feeding her—she was lonesome—and he had to go to work so he could get enough money to come back to Galveston and he knew that Greg wanted to hear how Riley was doing—Greg and all the neighbors, too. Everybody had been calling and they all wanted to know how Riley was and his father had to go back and bring the news and tell everyone all about the hospital, how it only had thirty beds in it, fifteen for the new kids and fifteen for kids who were in Reconstruction, the ones who were always flying up and down the halls and playing pool in the playroom, and about Dr. Walker and the nurses and everything that they were doing to put Riley back together. Riley's father said he would be back the next weekend and that he didn't know how he could stand it until then.

I already miss you and I already miss your mother and I haven't even left.

Riley could feel his father's head on the side of the bed. His father must have fallen asleep. He thought he might rest himself. He didn't want to think about his father leaving. It made him feel like he was disappearing down a long, dark hole. He was afraid he might leave himself. He was so glad his mother wasn't leaving but he didn't know if she would be enough to keep him here.

Riley?

Riley?

His father said that, while he was gone, Riley would have to take care of his mother. He said that all this—the fire and Riley hurting so bad and them not being sure about anything and coming to visit the hospital every day and having to talk to Dr. Walker and the nurses and being alone in the mother's dorm—was going to be very hard on her. He said that he knew that she would blame herself for the fire. He knew that because he knew the way she was.

You're a lot like your mother, sweetheart.

His father's breath was close to his head. *Riley? I don't want you to worry. I don't want you to stew. I just want you to get well.*

We'll take a vacation as soon as this is all over, I prom-

ise. We'll go camping. Maybe we'll meet up with some Indians who will teach us how to track big game—elk and grizzlies.

Riley slept a long while.

Riley? Are you listening? I need you to listen. I need you to pay attention. Please pay attention. This fire?—I might have done the very same thing when I was your age.

Riley dozed again while his father went on, something about how when he was growing up in Memphis when he was Riley's age he was playing with firecrackers and cherry bombs and throwing them in the toilet just for fun and how he was trying to shoot birds when he was a little older and then about his friend Jimmy Douglas and how Jimmy had done something or other with a gun and nearly lost his hand.

It's the sort of thing a boy will do. But your mother won't understand. You need to take care of her. Do you hear me, Riley? I want you to take care of your mother.

EVEN WHEN HE SLEPT, he knew his mother was there beside his bed, pasting cards in the little blue book. Or writing letters. Or putting everything that happened to him in a red notebook she'd bought at the grocery store. He could hear her pen as her hand moved across the page.

Even when he slept, he knew she was there, talking to Dr. Walker, talking to the nurses, talking to him, telling him every single thing, the sound of her voice a steady hum, like the waves against the beach in Galveston where she walked in the afternoons when she wasn't at the hospital.

Even when *she* slept, he knew she was there. He could hear her breathe, the steady rhythm of her snoring.

He missed his father, the weight of his father's hand on his feet.

4

Every day, the doctors and their students came and turned on the big light overhead and stood around his bed and talked about his last surgery—or his next surgery—and his face and what they were going to do to fix it and all sorts of things that seemed perfectly clear, their voices flashing through his mind like the goldfish skittering back and forth in the pond at the park around the corner from his house.

Sixty-three percent third-degree. People die of fluid loss people die of—bacterial invasion. Xeroflow. Polysporin. What's your rationale, Dr. Walker, as opposed to—? Chronic areas take too long. Intense inflammation, white cells fight, more of a problem in the—fungus. Nasal labial fold. Quality of life? What exactly will that be, Dr.—? God knows—

Sometimes they would ask him questions and he would answer right away and they would stand there with their faces looking worried and then Dr. Walker—who was a very tall man, with a single, long black hair coming from inside his thin nose—would lean down and say very loud, *We can't quite hear you, young man. Can you talk more clearly?* And then he would, even though the effort made his teeth chatter and his whole body start to tremble and the words came out all mixed up. But then Dr. Walker would come up real close to Riley with his face squeezed together hard, like he was trying to see something very far away.

It's all right, Riley, he would say. *Maybe later*.

THE MOTHER'S DORM was fine, his mother said. It was much better than the motel by the ocean. The mother's dorm was where she was living right now, where she would be for most of the week until his father got back. She missed his father very much. Before he came back, she would have to find something else, something better than a motel, maybe a boardinghouse. She'd heard there were some boardinghouses in Galveston, just for the families of people in the hospital. She would have to talk to the social worker, Melinda Kepler, to find out about one.

She said it was Melinda Kepler who had got her the bed in the mother's dorm because she had told Melinda they couldn't afford for her to stay in the Holiday Inn and that, once Riley's father left, she was afraid to stay in the motel by the ocean alone. The motel by the ocean had turned out to be a very bad place to stay. They had only seen it in the daylight. But at night, she said, at night when they went back to the motel after they left the hospital, after they left Riley, the fog came rolling in off the ocean and covered them so they thought they were swimming through gauzy white curtains. Up by the Seawall, the streetlights poked through the fog like little flashlights and suddenly that motel that had seemed so right that afternoon seemed dirty and dark and unsafe, like it was made out of matchsticks just waiting to be lit. Staying there didn't seem like such a good idea now that it was night. In that motel by the ocean, she said, people drank a lot of beer. She said you could see the cans and bottles lining up along the stairwells and walkways, and pizza boxes and all sorts of trash coming out of the garbage cans and the men and women who came there were too loud and the walls between the rooms were as thin as paper. That night, she said, there was so much laughing and shouting and the walls were so thin that it sounded as if the voices were coming up from underneath her bed. She sat up straight in her bed, her heart going so fast. She said right at that minute in the dark and in the middle of the night, with the drunken, wild voices seeming to enter her soul from the inside, she thought this is what hell must be like, especially when she remembered why they were in Galveston and that Riley was up here lying on his bed alone. She said there were cars whizzing by on the Seawall all night long, she could hear them, going so fast she couldn't keep track of them and she couldn't sleep and when she went down to the beach to walk early in the morning with Riley's father, there were cars driving on the beach just as if the beach was a road. She almost couldn't believe it.

She didn't even like to think about that motel by the ocean.

The mother's dorm where she was right now—even though she was alone—seemed just fine by comparison. The mother's dorm was convenient because it was right across the street from the hospital, but it was very small with only two bedrooms, two beds per bedroom, and one small kitchen and one little tiny living room with a TV you could hear all over the apartment. The two other mothers who lived there were always watching horrible movies on the TV—

One night they wanted to watch The Texas Chainsaw Massacre—

And staying up all night and laughing and talking so

much she couldn't think. Although I shouldn't be so hard on them, she said. They aren't new to this place like I am, she said. Maybe they had forgotten what it was like to have just arrived at the hospital. Maybe they hadn't realized that all she could think about was Riley. Maybe they had forgotten how much a person needed to talk or maybe they had talked so much about their own kids, they just decided to talk about everything else besides, including one other mother who was there but who was never there, a lady named Hattie who was the mother of a girl named Pat. They talked about Hattie all the time. Hattie is black, they told her, and the two other mothers were white and they felt the need to say every bad thing they could think of about her.

God almighty, Riley, she said, *we have landed in the South*.

His mother's voice drifted off, whispering.

Although God—if he was thinking about me at all—couldn't have sent me a better selection of roommates if he'd worked at it. They are different from me completely—no chance to find any sort of cultural sympathy. Rennie and Diane. They have thick Southern accents. They are both here for just about another week, though Rennie has been here a month and Diane for six weeks. Diane tells me she has had cancer three times, that she's at least fifty pounds overweight, has an underactive thyroid, her daughter's retarded, her son is burned, and that she went back home after a week to pack up and found her husband in bed with another woman—she tells me all this like she's won a contest with it!

Rennie and Diane took me to the store. They went past the fruit section and into the hot dog section really fast. They bought hot dogs and prepackaged chicken-fried steaks and a can of beans and frozen French fries, all of which they microwaved. They microwaved one of the hot dogs so long it looked like a burnt arm. Everything looks burnt. They smoke a lot of cigarettes and laugh a lot and talk about men all the time though they're married—well, maybe Diane isn't anymore—and they generally hate Hattie, who is the lady I share a bedroom with, who hasn't been here yet. According to them, she doesn't wash at all except for her face, which she washes with toilet paper. She wears black underwear—as if that's a crime. She is being sponsored by some church that is paying for her to stay at the Holiday Inn, but she is spending all of the money they give her for the Holiday Inn on new outfits and she is spending the night somewhere else entirely with some man, besides holding down a bed in the mother's dorm . . .

Well, she said out loud so that Riley heard her clearly,

maybe that is the only way to make yourself feel good, to spend all your money on new outfits. Maybe that's as good a therapy as any!

Rennie and Diane! They sit around all day talking talking talking about every single person who comes in here.

His mother's voice changed, as if she herself were in a Christmas play and had the role of one of the Wise Men—or someone else with a strange, squeaky voice—maybe Mary. *You seen that little negro boy? Don't have no mama. Mama done left. The daddy's girlfriend stuck that kid in a tub full of boiling water. She in jail for the rest of her life.*

And then another voice, deeper. *See that little-bitty baby? You seen that poor little baby by itself in the big room? Bless its heart. Its mama and daddy take drugs. Nurse said so—*

Back to the Mary voice. *Bless its heart. Bless its heart.*

And then her own. *Makes me sick—your grandmother from Memphis is always saying the same thing—bless his heart—bless his heart. Sounds exactly like a curse, like something you'd say to someone you hated!*

ONE NIGHT AT THE mother's dorm, she told him, she was lying in bed. It was late and it was dark and

Hattie still hadn't ever shown up and everybody was asleep, but she couldn't sleep and she was lying with her face to the window, which was right there next to her bed, and she was staring out her window into the pitch-dark night when suddenly there was a man on the other side of the window also lying down and staring right back at her. It was more than she could bear. And it was impossible! Because her room and that window were on the second floor of the building and no man, woman, or child could get up there to that window and lie down, unless there was some sort of ledge, but there wasn't, but she had seen it—a man staring straight back at her, the ugliest man she'd ever seen—just as surely as she had been transported by plane from El Paso to Galveston on a day when she had least expected it, exactly fourteen hours after Riley's fire.

She said she didn't like the mother's dorm at all, though she could see where somehow it might be good for her to be among so many people who were so different from her. But what she needed more than anything in the world was to be alone. She needed to be in a place where no one talked and there was no TV and she could write letters or write in her diary or talk on the phone without having to whisper, a place that Riley's father could come to and stay with her on the weekends when he was able to fly back to Galveston. She needed to eat vegetables and a salad. Right now she would not touch a hot dog if it was the last thing on earth she had to eat. She needed to keep herself strong. She needed to walk. She needed to climb the stairs and not even be tempted to take the elevators, which is what her roommates in the mother's dorm always did.

I've got to stay strong, Riley. I've just got to stay strong.

5

Two men they called the tub men came every morning except the mornings after he had his surgeries. They said their names were Jackson and Johnson. Jackson was a skinny old man, pitch-black, with gray hair and a bumpy line between his nose and his upper lip, which seemed to be stuck on one of his teeth. He wore thick black glasses. Johnson was the biggest man Riley had ever seen and had a smile that went from one side of his face to the other with lots and lots of big white teeth in between. He called everybody *honey*, just like Riley's father had told him people in Galveston did. When Jackson and Johnson came to get Riley, they took him down the hall to the elevator and down the elevator to the tub room, which was all white with bright lights and a big, shiny steel tub in the middle. They took off his hospital gown and they unwrapped all his bandages—*You cold, now, honey?—Don't you worry, this tub will be all nice and warm, we* *got the water running all nice and warm just for you, don't we, Jackson—yes sir, we do, nice and warm—yes sir, you get that water all nice and warm for this Riley, otherwise he be complaining and wanting to leave us, can't have that, got to treat our boy Riley just right—* and soaked off his gauze and picked at him to get rid of his dead skin, and told jokes and made all sorts of noises.

Now, Riley, they always said just before they put him in the tub, *this is going to hurt a little bit* and then his whole body would tense up and as soon as he hit the water, he felt like he was on fire again. There was no relief from it. The minute the tub men came in the door of his room to get him, his mother was standing up so quick and pushing back her chair and moving out of the room as if she was in everyone's way. There was all kinds of screaming, he couldn't help himself *can't you wait can't you wait another day I don't need a bath* he cried out but the whole effort made him tremble and his voice wouldn't come out loud enough for anyone to hear or listen to and his mother—who might have been able to save him—had disappeared and then the nurses were moving all around his bed, fluttering, their voices high and loud and telling him he was going to be all right.

Which he knew wasn't true.

The tub men never paid a bit of attention to him, they

just kept laughing and talking, Jackson starting in to say something over against Johnson's conversation, Johnson replying before Jackson had finished. The air around them was filled with their deep humming, their okaying and uh-huhing and yeah-boys. Not even a minute of silence prevailed when the tub men came around. Except when they first put him in the tub and then they would shut up, looking and looking, Jackson squinting through his glasses, his neck stuck out like an old crow's, deep sighs but no words, assessing where to begin to poke and prod. And then the talking started right up again.

Hey, Riley, you hear about that rooster wanting to cross the road. You know why? You know why, Riley?

He knew why. Of course he knew why. That was an old joke, the dumb kind kids in kindergarten thought was so funny. He tried to tell the tub men that he was going to be in second grade and that he already knew the answer, but Johnson right away called out, *Had to get to the other side, yeah-boy!*

Then quick as you please, Jackson said, *You like them knock-knock jokes, Riley? You got any of them knock-knock jokes for us?*

How about poems, Riley? You got any poems? Jackson loves a good poem.

Riley didn't think he knew any poems, at least not

right then, not when he was holding himself so tight against the pain and every sound the tub men made seemed to just add to it. He didn't want them to talk or to ask any more questions or to touch him, but they went right on doing those very things, not caring much if Riley said a word, until finally Johnson leaned over and said, *Hey, Riley, did you know that God's first name is Andy?*

Riley hadn't thought too much about God and certainly not enough to know that God had a first name or even what it was and then he couldn't tell if this was just another joke and they were just pulling his leg or if the tub men really knew for a fact about God's first name. But they didn't seem to care what Riley thought because they just started singing suddenly, swaying back and forth a little, their voices as low as any he'd ever heard.

And He walks with me,
And He talks with me,
And He tells me I am His own—
And the joy we share as we tarry there,
None other has ever known.

Do you get it, Riley? Jackson asked when they had finished. *And-y walks with me, And-y talks with me*—and they started singing again.

Riley didn't get it, but the sound of their voices, so incredibly rich and deep, made him relax suddenly and he peed in the water.

Ohhhh, said Jackson. *I knew we was good but I didn't know we was that good!* And then the whole room rang around with laughter and talk, which Riley didn't quite appreciate since it was all at his expense.

They had to drain the water and start again, and while they were doing that, Riley realized he did know a poem, one his father had taught him.

Fat and Skinny had a race
Up and down the pillow case
Fat fell down and broke his face
And Skinny said, "I won the race!"

He said it in his mind. As soon as he could, he would teach the Fat and Skinny poem to the tub men. Then, if there were any other kids who got baths, the tub men could tell it to them and could tell them that they had heard it first from Riley Martin, a new boy who had come from El Paso.

But, really—just like with almost everything—he forgot the Fat and Skinny poem for a long time—forgot to tell it to the tub men and then even forgot the poem itself.

6

Riley!

His mother's voice was louder than usual and she was leaning way down close to his face. *This is Uncle Neale. He is your Grandfather Grider's brother. I just met him myself. I never met him before today. Can you imagine? He heard about you and drove all the way over here from Kansas.*

His mother put her arm around an old man who pushed his face into a smile. *Riley! Are you awake?* his mother said. *I'm going to let Uncle Neale have a little time alone with you. I'm going to go talk to Marilyn Hooper.*

The door shut. Then Uncle Neale cleared his throat and reintroduced himself. He asked if Riley could hear him and Riley said yes, but it seemed like Uncle Neale hadn't understood because he leaned in closer and squinted his eyes together and then just as quickly backed off, like a person does when they get too close to a fart. He folded his arms across his chest and stared at Riley for a while, and then sat down and then stood up again and then in what seemed like a whisper he began to tell Riley how he had heard about him and about the fire and how it was a shame and how he hated the whole thing and how he hated fire and how he'd never met Riley's mother, his niece, but was glad to have the chance to meet her now though he was sorry about the circumstances and then he began to tell Riley about the trip from Kansas down through Texas and on into Galveston and where he had spent the night and about the changes in weather and scenery and about how big Texas was and about how he hadn't known that and about many other things all in a quiet voice without breaks except that in what seemed like the middle of everything he cleared his throat again and then leaned over to get his jacket and left. The door shut behind him.

THE NURSES CAME IN and out of his room all day and all night. *Turn over, you got to turn over, Riley. Sit up, Riley, you got to sit up. Open your mouth, Riley, you got to open your mouth.*

Sometimes they made his mother leave, especially when he was crying or she was crying. He knew each one of their voices. Each voice had a smell attached to it and a certain touch though he had not yet been able to locate every face—except for a few.

One was a lady who reminded him of home the way she talked. Her name was Miss Miranda. She was short and always wore a mask over her face and a cap on her head and her hands were very kind.

Another was a tall black man named Gene, the one who called his father honey. He told Riley that the minute he got some time he was going to come to El Paso to buy a pair of lizard-skin boots.

But the one he remembered the most was an old man with big red glasses and popped-out eyes and crooked teeth and white hair that stuck straight up, with a voice like a broken plate. When he was in the room, everything got bigger and louder. If he came in the room when Riley's mother was there, she always stood up and started apologizing, as if she was in the way.

His name was Mr. Loflin and he had been in the army and his voice was always demanding that you do something and he pushed and shoved and poked and pulled and never stopped moving and wanted everything to be yes sir and no sir and square corners and do it right the first time and he talked and talked when he was in the room, yelling and yelling like Riley was halfway across the moon.

7

His mother kept asking him did he remember the plane ride, but he didn't have the energy to answer and he didn't remember anyway. So she told him. More than once.

It was one of those scenes you imagine danger and adventure in, but never yourself—like out of a movie. It was five-thirty in the morning, she said. Vicki stood at the front door. She had spent the night there with them, to help them, because so much was happening. They had one suitcase, filled with clothes that didn't match. She couldn't think to make things go together and nothing they had ever went together anyway.

I do not like the early morning dark, she told him. *People should be asleep in the darkness in their beds with their dreams.*

She said they had sat in the family waiting room at the hospital in El Paso all afternoon and on into the night, waiting for the doctors to bring them news about Riley. When the news finally came, it wasn't good.

They had to get you here to Galveston right away, that's what the doctor said. Because here in Galveston they know how to treat children who are burned and they can do it better than they can there in El Paso.

They told them to go home and get packed and get some sleep, that they would start looking for a private plane right away that could take Riley first thing in the morning, but that his mother and father would have to get a commercial plane and get there themselves. *Just the thought of being separated from you nearly killed me.*

But they hardly slept. The phone rang all night, a thousand people calling. Marie Mangas and Sarah Orton and Joe and Jill. The neighbors came over and stood around the dining room table and watched them eat. They didn't have anything to say. Neither did his mother and father. Then the hospital called—it was all about the plane—*we can't get a plane.* Then they called again. *We can get a plane, but it's only big enough for the mother to come.* But finally the hospital called and they had a plane big enough for all of them, for Riley and his mother and father and two nurses and a man who sat there and smiled and brought them juice and coffee and a deck of cards—*as if we wanted to play cards!*—a private jet donated by the local gas company.

She got out of bed at four o'clock. She couldn't sleep. She put their stuff in a suitcase. She made Riley's bed and cleaned his room. She didn't know what else to do with herself. Lady Luck was asleep in the little, soft hole underneath the Mexican elder in the backyard.

The neighborhood was completely quiet. The early morning dark was like a blanket over it. The mountains at the top of the street were just shadows, silent and sleeping, like big cats. Tom and Ginny and the girls were still sleeping, Bertha and Arturo, all the Favelas. There was a light on in Mrs. Pino's kitchen across the street. They found out later that she was sitting by her radio, listening for news about Riley, and how they would get him to Galveston.

His father backed the old car out of the driveway, lights on, down the empty street, past the yellow glare of the 7-Eleven, down Piedras to Montana. They got lost, looking for the gas company's hangar. They parked the car inside the gate. On the runway, there was a little plane with its lights on and its propellers whirring and there were men walking around below it wearing red hats with tassels on them and business suits. It was five in the morning and completely dark and there they were, the Shriners, all dressed up in their fezzes like they were going to be in a parade.

His mother and father walked out toward the plane. His mother didn't know where Riley was. She thought he was already in the plane. The Shriners all shook their hands. They were very serious.

Hello, hello, are you Riley's parents? That's what the Shriners asked his mother and father. One of them said, *You must be torn up*, in such a way that she felt like he knew every feeling she was having. It seemed like the nicest thing anyone had ever said.

The Shriners said they were just waiting for the ambulance to bring Riley from the hospital and then the plane would take off. His mother was shivering. *I was afraid that you would come and I was afraid that you would never come,* she said. *Either way I was afraid. I don't like the dark, Riley, and the airplane in the dark with its engine going and its lights on and the men in suits with red hats walking around beneath it frightened me so I couldn't stop shaking.* My wife is cold, his father told them. One of the men took his mother inside the hangar where there was a heated office, but still she kept shivering.

Then the sun started coming up at the edge of the desert, coming up along the tops of the mountains.

And then the ambulance appeared, creeping across the field, its lights on, pushing through the darkness.

And you were in it and I was afraid to see you—so afraid, she said and didn't talk for a long time.

• • •

Riley?

Are you sure you don't remember the airplane, Riley? You don't remember those two nurses, the fat one with the big bosom who kept teasing you and talking to you? You don't remember us telling you about seeing Galveston from the air, about seeing all the water?

What about the ambulance ride down by the Seawall?

Well, he wouldn't have seen anything. He was in the back, lying down and his face and his head were already swollen as big as a balloon, his eyes completely shut. His father sat back there with him and his mother was up front with the ambulance driver, a lady, and she was telling his mother all about Galveston, the last really bad hurricane and the Seawall and the beaches and the places to eat and shop—

Just like we were coming for a vacation—

8

Riley?

I've found the perfect place. I had to find a place because your father will be back this weekend to stay with me. I've already moved in.

The place his mother had found was a boardinghouse owned by an old lady who wore sneakers and a man's shirt and dungarees and worked in her garden. The lady's name was Mrs. Griswald and she had a friend named Arnold who spent his days at the flea market. She said that Arnold's car was always filled up with junk he'd bought one day and intended to sell the next.

His mother said that in her new apartment, which was on the third floor of Mrs. Griswald's boardinghouse, she was completely on her own. She could eat what she wanted and sleep all night long. There were no cars rushing by outside. The boardinghouse was not too far from the ocean, and only a short walk from the hospital. There was no TV and there was a big bed for her and Riley's father when he was there and another smaller bed for when visitors like Grandma or maybe her friend Betsy came and outside her windows were the tops of Mrs. Griswald's magnolia trees. She could see them. If she opened the windows, she could almost touch them. She said it was like living in a tree house.

It's like sleeping on a screened-in porch, like the one we had right off my brother's bedroom in the house where I grew up in New Jersey. It's that peaceful.

GRANDMA IS HERE, RILEY. Come all the way from Memphis.

Riley? Can you say hello?

Grandma sucked her breath in really hard. *Bless his heart*, she said.

There was a problem with Grandma here, he knew, though he couldn't quite put his finger on what it was. Grandma kept asking his mother questions. One was, Why wouldn't his mother take an afternoon off and drive up to Houston to have dinner? Another was, Why had Riley set the fire? Why? she kept saying. Why and how come? Was he unhappy? It made his mother cry.

She asked Riley questions, too, when his mother was in the bathroom or downstairs to get some coffee. He felt that he answered them all very clearly, but Grandma just kept asking, leaning over to press them into his face.

He was glad to see her come, but, for his mother's sake—and for his own—he was happier when she left.

RILEY?

He felt his father's hand on his foot. *Oh, honey,* he said, *I'm back. I'm so glad to be back.* He brought news from home—everybody and his brother had either called or stopped by the house to find out about Riley. All eight of the Favelas had come down at one time or another with the same question: How is Riley? When's he coming home? All the people at Riley's father's job had taken him out to lunch his first day back and sat around looking so sad, it made Riley's father want to cry. Everybody was thinking about them and praying for Riley. Greg had come down with his mother. Greg looked terrible, Riley's father reported. His hair was sticking up on end, and it was obvious that Greg wasn't holding up well under the strain of Riley's absence. Riley's teacher, Mrs. Althoff, had brought over a bunch of get-well cards the kids in his class had made and as soon as Riley was able, they would look them all over.

The *El Paso Times* had reported that the Diablos were just warming up at the Dudley Dome. Someone—he didn't know who—maybe somebody from his job—had told the Diablos that Riley would be back in time for the opening pitch. That would be the first thing they'd do when Riley got home, his father said. They would go to the Dudley Dome just like before. They would take Greg with them—have twenty-five-cent hot dogs and fifty-cent cups of Coke and—probably some beer and—the announcer would call out Riley's name and everyone would wave to him as he stood up in the stands—because the Diablos—and most of El Paso—knew that Riley was in the hospital and would be home soon—

9

After a while they moved Riley out of the room where he was alone and into Room 312. Room 312 was a big room with four beds, two of them empty until Riley came along. Carnell Hughes was in one of them and a little girl named LaKeesha in the other. LaKeesha was always coming up close to Riley, her elbow on his bed, and whispering to him about a girl she had seen named Pat who everybody knew was the meanest and ugliest girl in the whole, wide world—Mr. Loflin said so—whose color had all been burned off and how Pat had a mother named Hattie with a face like a pig and long earrings that jingled who was a midnight dancer and how she had an uncle named Jimmy that no one had ever seen but who had killed a man and how Pat was always screaming out his name *Jimmy Jimmy Jimmy* and how Pat had poured too much gasoline on the barbecue just because she was mad at her mother's new boyfriend and how Pat cried and cried and said they had stolen all her fingers and how she wanted them back, but it wasn't true because those fingers came off in the fire which she started her own self—LaKeesha hadn't started her own fire, the hot-water heater blew up—and how Pat was crazy and how LaKeesha wished that Pat would *die* she was so mean and so ugly! *I hates her!* LaKeesha whispered. *I hates her! She's the world's biggest crybaby. When you sees her lying in the playroom, you can't tell if you are looking at a boy or a girl. Looks like a black thing covered with chalk. You just waits till you see her—*

Riley didn't yet have the strength to care one way or the other about Pat, but the whispering and the hot, sour smell of LaKeesha's breath and the news that it brought seemed to knit itself right into his skin.

And there was Mr. Loflin again, bustling into Room 312 and crying out in a voice that seemed to cut right to his insides. *Well, here's Mr. Riley Martin! So they put you in the biiig room, did they! Here you are with my little gal LaKeesha!*

LaKeesha said so bright and proud, Why, Mr. Loflin, here I is! What you know about that Pat? How's that mean and ugly girl?

Oh, sweetheart, you don't know how mean—spits her food in your face when you try to feed her. Rubs her skin so bad none of them grafts can stay in place. We're going to have to tie that mean girl's hands down. And you know what else? She pees all over herself the minute they give her a bath.

Silly girl, said LaKeesha.

Apple don't fall too far from the tree, hear? Her mother comes in swinging those long earrings of hers back and forth, cussing and carrying on, and the first thing she says to that girl is—Mr. Loflin put on a high squeaky voice—*You probably gonna die. You gonna be in the hospital forever. You gonna have a bunch of operations. When they finish with you, you gonna be ugly.*

Ohhhh, she's ugly all right, said LaKeesha. What apple you mean?

LAKEESHA HAD A BIG, pink piggy bank. Her pig, she called it.

A whole bunch of people who knew her were standing outside the window one Saturday morning and looking in, tapping on the window and wiggling their fingers and waving dollar bills at her. An old man in overalls shuffled into the room with a ten-dollar bill between his fingers and tried to stick it into LaKeesha's pig but not before LaKeesha's grandmother fussed at him saying for sure it would get stolen, that someone would steal little

LaKeesha's pig right off her nightstand. *Not a soul could be trusted in this whole hospital—*

The nurse was changing Riley's bandages and had left him naked on his bed, and another one of LaKeesha's visitors, a very tall, skinny man with gold chains around his neck and gold caps on his teeth, came in and grabbed the remote control off of Riley's nightstand and started changing the channels, settling finally on a show called *Soul Train* and turning the sound up really loud and dancing all over the room. Riley's mother put a sheet over Riley and then asked the man to give the remote control back and the man yelled *Keep your hands off me!* The nurse came in and his mother was crying but Riley could hardly hear her for the noise from the TV and all the confusion.

But he didn't remember too much about all that either.

Things didn't really start to come into focus until much later, long after LaKeesha had left for good, and it was just him and Carnell Hughes and then Parker MacGwyn, who came into Room 312 wearing not a hospital gown but blue-striped pajamas from home, and sitting in a wheelchair pushed by his father and his mother—whose perfume entered the door with her—Mr. and Mrs. Kingsley MacGwyn of Baton Rouge, Louisiana.

But—really—it wasn't until two weeks after that, when Melvin Pitts arrived to fill up the fourth bed in Room 312, that Riley Martin began to come back to his old self—that old self who was so earnest, so densely considerate, so quick to be hurt and so slow to respond, the old self who took life so seriously, who was so demanding in some ways, so determined in others, who loved to talk, who worried and dreamed and stewed about everything and thought everything over all the time.

10

During the time that Riley Martin, Carnell Hughes, Parker MacGwyn, and Melvin Pitts were in Room 312, Parker's mother—Corliss to Riley's mother, Miss MacGwyn to everyone else—did all the talking and rule-making while Parker MacGwyn always picked the TV shows the room would watch because Parker was the oldest and Parker had the remote control on his nightstand. Even though Riley was able to recite the day and time of every program and Carnell Hughes had certain babyish preferences, it was always Parker who decided what shows the room would watch and it was always Melvin Pitts who was bad and the butt of all their jokes.

Riley Martin liked Carnell Hughes okay except that Carnell was only four and too young—at least for him—to really play with, but Riley worshipped Parker MacGwyn because he was a teenager.

And at first Riley had liked Melvin Pitts because Melvin

was a mysteriously big boy like himself. But then—almost right away—Riley didn't like Melvin Pitts because Riley was quickly repulsed by all the horrifying big-boy things that Melvin did.

Melvin Pitts was always whining, for one thing. He was always talking and talking—so much that you couldn't think—insisting that whatever Riley said was wrong—and he was always standing too close to Riley's bed and he was clumsy and he tripped *all* the time because he didn't know where his feet were and he always came crashing out of his bed as if he'd been struck by lightning and he farted out loud without being the least bit ashamed. And his farts smelled terrible! Riley figured that Melvin might have been twelve. Or fifteen. But he was probably nine or maybe seven—just like Riley.

But Riley didn't know for sure because Melvin Pitts, when he first arrived at the hospital, didn't have a mother and father on the scene to explain who he was or to be used as a reference point or to give him a hand or to stick up for him. Melvin Pitts just seemed to appear out of nowhere, as if he'd been dropped off at the hospital's door.

Carnell Hughes didn't have a mother or a father either, only an old grandmother who came to visit on Saturdays with a paper bag full of candy corn and a mouth full of sad stories, but Carnell Hughes was easier to figure out than Melvin Pitts.

Whenever Melvin Pitts got out of hand, Parker MacGwyn would say, MEEEL-vin, stop your whining.

Parker's mother would repeat Parker's command: Melvin, stop your whining, would you *please*? You are not allowed to whine anymore! No one in Room 312 is allowed to whine!

Then Melvin would spit out, I don't like Parker. I don't like what he says to me.

Which would make Parker's mother mad. Parker says what YOU need to hear, Melvin Pitts, she would say.

Yes, Melvin Pitts, Parker would always say, I say just what YOU need to hear.

Riley would try to think of something to say to Melvin that would catch his attention and cause him to stop acting so silly and bothering Parker and causing Parker's mother to get so upset. *Just stay out of it*, his own mother would hiss at him whenever Parker and Miss MacGwyn talked to Melvin like that—as if she knew exactly what Riley was thinking!—and she'd keep her arms folded over her stomach until they quit.

Then Melvin would suddenly fling a complaint willy-nilly out into the room. I can't read in cursive. I hate cursive, I can't read in it and I can't write in it. NA NA NA NA NA NA NA.

Cut it out, Melvin, Parker would say. Those are my greeting cards you're trying to read. They are none of your business.

Parker MacGwyn's nightstand was filled with—besides the remote control and a dozen fancy greeting cards—candy, baseball cards, and a photo of Erik Estrada from the TV show *CHiPs* signed *To Parker, Hope you get better soon, Buddy*, with a flourishing signature—in cursive—from the man himself.

Five o'clock p.m. would come around and Riley would opt for *Wonder Woman* with Carnell Hughes in agreement, but Melvin would whine that he never got a chance to pick anything and that he was always being pushed around by everybody and that nobody liked him or wanted to be his friend and that he needed a best friend bad—every day the same complaint.

Oh shut up, Melvin, you big baby, Parker would say, holding the remote control in his hands. Nobody even wants to be your friend, let alone your best friend.

Melvin, Parker's mother would say, you are acting like a big baby. We do not appreciate it when you act like a baby.

I want a chance to pick the show! Melvin would cry out. I want to have the remote control on my nightstand!

You can't, she said. Oh forever, no. That's against the rules. We'd all go perfectly crazy!

Turn it to *Wonder Woman*, Carnell Hughes would fret. We missing the whole thing.

Hurry, said Riley Martin, it's already begun.

Give me that thing, Melvin would say, grabbing for the remote.

Parker's mother would stand up then and take the remote control from Parker. I'll change the channels, Melvin, she would say, and you show me what you want. Click click click click, went the remote control in Miss MacGwyn's long hands with the red fingernails. The gold bracelets on her arm jingled back and forth. Tell me when, Melvin, she'd say, and she'd open her eyes very wide and stare at him over the eyeglasses that sat on the end of her nose.

There! Melvin Pitts would sing out, just as soon as Wonder Woman appeared on the screen in her tall boots.

Oh, you fussbudget, Parker's mother would say. That's where we were going in the first place. Stop your whining, Melvin Pitts.

You're the pits, Melvin, Parker MacGwyn would then declare.

You *are* the pits, Riley Martin would echo with solemn conviction.

You should talk, Riley, Melvin would shoot right back at him.

Riley!—came quickly from under his mother's breath. *Stop this minute!*

Yeees, Carnell Hughes—without a mother there to correct him—would giggle in his tiny, trembly voice, *you* the pits, Melvin.

11

From the minute he met him, Riley spent a lot of time thinking about Melvin Pitts. There was something so familiar about him. But then, right away, that which was familiar became too familiar. And then, right away, Riley began to listen to other people's opinions. And other people—*many* other people—thought that Melvin was the pits. *A big boy who acted like a baby*, is what they said—the same difficult thing that Riley had heard about himself all his life.

Even Melvin's father—Harry—who came to visit him only once—agreed. Harry Pitts looked just like his son: fat, with eyebrows that sloped down towards his cheeks. He kept wiping his face off with a big, wet handkerchief. He talked and talked—just like Melvin—mostly to Parker's father, Mr. MacGwyn, but hardly to Melvin.

Melvin's father's excuse for not coming to stay with Melvin in the beginning was that he was in the produce business, and when the produce was ready to move, he had to move it. He didn't barely have a minute to come over and visit Melvin, who, he said, was forever getting into one scrape or another. And his wife couldn't come because they had five other kids!

Harry said that Melvin had managed to get himself to the hospital because he was trying to kill his little brother, and in doing so, he fell backward onto the stove and burned his back and then his side and his hand.

Melvin is nine, Mr. Pitts said, in answer to that question from Kingsley MacGwyn.

Though he has the mouth of a fifteen-year-old and acts like a baby, Mr. Pitts added.

Even Melvin's father thought he was the pits!

Riley, then just seven years old, didn't like Melvin's jokes. They were full of words that Riley didn't understand, though Parker MacGwyn, nearly fourteen, laughed at them loudly when his mother wasn't in the room. Riley didn't like the way Melvin Pitts pretended to want to watch something different whenever Parker turned on *Wonder Woman* or the way he accused them all of only wanting to watch that show because of Lynda Carter's tits, a word Riley heard for the first time out of Melvin Pitts' mouth.

Riley didn't like the way Melvin called him Liar either.

Hey, Liar, Melvin said to him, leaning up too close against Riley's bed whenever Riley's mother wasn't around.

I'm not a liar, Melvin, Riley would protest.

You are too a liar, Liar, Melvin would accuse him. You told me you were the boy in the picture. You lied to me.

Melvin was talking about a photo that had been on Riley's nightstand, a photo that Riley's father had sent from El Paso so that Riley could show it to the doctors and nurses. Riley was proud of that photo, taken right at the beginning of first grade. He'd sat up especially straight that day, made his mother let him wear the red-plaid flannel shirt that was his favorite and looked right into the camera without blinking.

Who's this, Riley? Melvin asked him on the day when he first moved into Room 312.

That's me, Riley had replied.

That's not you! Melvin had screamed out like he was in pain. You're lying to me. You don't look anything like that. You look like a monster!

Right away Riley's mother gave Melvin a terrible look. Riley knew that in a minute she was going to start crying.

He should look in the mirror, Melvin yelled at her. He could see for himself.

But there were no mirrors in Room 312.

Riley's mother took the photo and put it in her purse.

No, really, Melvin kept on doggedly. You should get him a mirror, he really needs to look at himself in the mirror, you should get him one . . .

Riley could see that Melvin just wasn't going to quit, at least not until Riley's mother had started to cry for sure. An idea flashed into his head—a possible distraction—and—in a panic and without thinking—he gave it a tentative try.

Hey, Melvin, he mumbled, trying to sound cheerful, *did you know that God's first name is Andy?*

Melvin shut his eyes hard and scrunched up his neck. *Andy!* he howled. His eyes popped open. *God's first name is Andy? What are you talking about? How do you know that? God doesn't have a first name! Who told you God had a first name? My mother would kill you if she heard you talking like that!*

Melvin's response took the wind out of Riley's punch line, which really wasn't much of a punch line at all since he still didn't know if this business about God's first name was a joke and he, for sure, didn't know the song that somehow seemed to explain it. He'd definitely backed himself into a corner.

Nonetheless, the question served its purpose. It made Melvin forget about the photo and the mirrors.

At least until the next day. First thing in the morning he wanted to know where the picture of Riley was. When Riley asked his mother about it, she said she had taken it back to her apartment and then she folded her arms up over her chest in a way that meant it was going to stay there. When Riley asked her if she had gotten him a mirror, she just blinked her eyes, sucked her lips together, and stared straight ahead as if she hadn't heard him.

12

Parker MacGwyn was haughty toward Melvin all the time and didn't cut him any slack. If Riley even dared suggest that Melvin get a break, Parker MacGwyn would laugh at him. Parker's mother would say that Melvin didn't deserve a thing, especially a break, and that the best thing to do with Melvin was to just ignore him. Then she and Parker would do just that. Then Riley would pick up a book, trying to hide behind it and look busy, knowing what was coming next.

Then Melvin Pitts would have a howling fit, screaming that he needed someone to play with. Come on, Riley, he would whine. Come with me to the playroom. I need someone to come with me.

I'm busy, Riley would say, staring even harder at his book.

And then Riley's mother would say that Riley was not busy at all, that he had, in fact, been saying he was so bored, and she would insist that Riley and Melvin go down to the playroom, and down they would go, followed by Carnell Hughes with Riley's mother close behind. Riley hated to be seen with Melvin Pitts! And his mother knew it. He would have turned around in a second if she wasn't there with her hand on his shoulder.

The tub men told Riley that Melvin was too big—*a big old boy*, they said—no matter how old he was and that he fought them like the devil himself when they tried to give him a bath and he wouldn't stop ruckusing around and crying out in that croaky-boy voice of his when they tried to clean him up and that he was all the time cursing them with ugly words—*ooohheee, boy, like nothing you ever heard in your whoole lifetime! And he SCREAMS when we start singing!*

The nurses got mad at Melvin because he was always arguing and because he was always crying for them to settle his arguments and because he peed in his bed at night. That made them really mad! Are you a baby? Mr. Loflin always screeched at him when he discovered Melvin's wet sheets.

When Riley's father came to visit on the weekend after Melvin Pitts arrived and saw what was going on in Room 312, he had a very long talk with Riley. He told Riley that he thought Melvin Pitts was the sort of boy who attracted trouble. Trouble is Melvin's karma, is exactly what Riley's father told him. *It's the type of thing that takes several lifetimes to change.* He told Riley that he knew the situation in Room 312 wasn't easy, but—even so—he wanted Riley to treat Melvin Pitts as kindly as possible. *You don't know what Melvin Pitts is going through—and—you don't know when you might go through the same thing yourself—people not understanding you,* his father said.

Riley knew that all this was true. He held on tight to his very best behavior toward Melvin Pitts until Sunday afternoon when his father flew back to El Paso. Then he lay in bed trying to measure the words "as kindly as possible" against his own behavior toward Melvin. He always came up short! His heart betrayed him—he couldn't stand Melvin Pitts!

And Parker's father—well, Parker's father, Kingsley, was, according to Riley's mother, the cause of the whole problem in the first place.

According to Riley's mother, it was Kingsley MacGwyn who first met Melvin in the playroom shortly after Melvin arrived from Arkansas. Melvin was crying and crying. He was in a room with some other boys who treated him bad, he sobbed to anyone who would listen. It was Kingsley who first felt sorry for Melvin because of

Melvin's pitiful tears and it was Kingsley who—without thinking about it—took that as a sign that Melvin was upset because his parents weren't with him and because the boys in his room weren't kind, and not because Melvin was by nature the pits. And it was Kingsley who asked the head nurse if Melvin could be put in Room 312, instead of the mean-boy room he was in, so Melvin could be with Parker—*such a good influence*—and with Riley Martin and 'the *little* negro boy Carnell' and so that Kingsley himself and his wife could keep an eye out for the poor boy, but it was Kingsley's own son who was the meanest to Melvin and Kingsley's own wife—Parker's mother—who wasn't much help either as far as being nice went.

Parker's mother didn't care to lie. That's what she always told everyone. Oh, I can't stand him, she would say about Melvin right in front of him. Oh, Kingsley, she would whine to Kingsley the minute he walked in, now we're all up in arms over Melvin. She would tell Riley's mother that people who came from Arkansas generally had no manners and that she knew that Melvin Pitts's family was just trash—*I cannot think of any other word to describe them*—imagine his mother and father not even being here to stay by his side! Imagine a big boy who still urinated in his bed! Who used profanity with the tub men and the nurses!

Riley Martin could tell by the scowl on his mother's face and the way she folded her arms over her stomach that this problem with Melvin in particular and everything about Room 312 in general was driving her crazy, not to mention the fact that she didn't seem to like Parker's mother at all, even though they talked half the day away, his mother saying things he couldn't make sense of in a whispery unnatural voice that seemed more like Parker's mother's than her own, and staring at Parker's mother with her eyes open so wide it looked like she was going to cry whenever Parker's mother was talking—which is just about all Parker's mother ever did—going on and on about her *muuther* and daddy and her wonderful family and about how they spent *all* their Christmases at the Broooadmoor Hotel in Colorado Springs with their own *huge* Christmas tree in their rooms—they had their own suite—*I have such wonderful memories of my childhood!*—and about what a wonderful wonderful boy Parker was and how everyone in Baton Rouge knew Kingsley's family—and hers too—*after all, our families have lived in Baton Rouge forever!*

Now, where did you say El Paso is? she was always asking his mother. *Why, we'll just have to stop over there on our way up to the Springs one Christmas!*

It seemed to Riley that his mother wasn't happy at all. When she looked at him, she frowned right away, coming forward to fuss and frump with the sheets on his bed or to tug at his pajamas and she stared at his face for long periods of time without once looking in his eyes, just as if she'd been hypnotized by an invisible magician.

When they were alone—which wasn't often—she told Riley that there was not a thing she could do about Melvin Pitts and that she was not going to ask to have Riley put in another room because that wasn't the answer and that Riley was going to have to do his best with what he had and that Parker MacGwyn was just a spoiled brat—he was hardly even burned at all—she was sure that his ankle caught on fire because he was drinking and smoking cigarettes—*even though he is their precious darling boy,* she spit out—and that the MacGwyns put on airs because they thought they were somebody and thought they had all the answers and thought they were better parents than anyone else because they were from Louisiana, and because Kingsley didn't have to work for a living because he'd inherited a fortune and the Cadillac dealership in Baton Rouge and wore tasseled loafers without socks and Bermuda shorts and because Parker's mother always wore pearls and yellow cashmere sweaters and expensive perfume—*I hate that perfume it makes me want to throw up it smells like bug spray I'm going to tell her any day now that it makes me sick and ask her not to wear it*—and bright-red lipstick and matching fingernail polish and had enough money to get those nails done at the beauty parlor every week.

That's how Southern people are, Riley, she said. *I know. Your father and I lived in Memphis the first year we were married—and got out of there as fast as we could.*

She personally couldn't understand why Kingsley had brought Melvin Pitts into Room 312 in the first place. He may be rich, she told Riley, but he doesn't have any sense. He should have known better.

Any fool could tell just by looking at Melvin Pitts that he was trouble, she added—*a boy that big acting like such a baby!* She flushed all red up around her neck the minute she said that, then shut her eyes tight and stopped talking.

The whole situation made Riley's stomach a wreck. That and the fact that the strawberry milk they had served him one day as a treat had made him throw up. It made him so sick that he asked to have the word spread among the nurses that he could only have white milk on his tray, no other. He told the tub men about it, too. But even so, the memory of the strawberry milk lived on intensely in different unexpected sights and places, like in the elevator on the way to the tubs or passing through the hallway on the way to the playroom or looking through the long, skinny windows in that same corridor out toward the ocean. Had someone else who'd also drunk strawberry milk thrown up there?

13

Other times when they were alone, Riley's mother would start talking about Galveston and the ocean and the beach and how she was always walking along beside it when she wasn't at the hospital and that would naturally get her talking about Lavallette.

Lavallette was the name of the town on the New Jersey shore that his mother had gone to every summer for three weeks in August when she was growing up. It was close to a place called Seaside Heights, and his mother's family rented a little cottage there, a cozy place with beds built into the walls on the screened-in porch and every morning her mother—Riley's New Jersey grandmother—took her and her brothers and sister to the bay to swim and then right after lunch they all went up to the ocean and her mother sat directly on the sand in a little folding chair with no legs and she read a book and her nose was white with thick suntan cream and she always wore sunglasses. Her father—Riley's grandfather, a silent man—only came to the ocean at five p.m. He was very fair and not given to sitting in the sun or to reading on the beach or to flinging himself into the waves or to lying belly down in the sand to warm up after an hour in the water. Instead he came at five p.m. to take his exercise, which consisted of steady laps he swam parallel to the beach.

The beaches were very clean in New Jersey and not a soul would have ever dreamed of driving a car on them, ever—

Not like the beaches here in Galveston, Riley. They drive cars on the beaches here!

She'd told him the stories about Lavallette so many times when he was little, he knew them by heart. Riley himself had been there when he was a baby and again when he was four, she said, though he didn't remember, and he'd sat there on the sand and let the ocean curl up around his feet, and his grandmother and his grandfather had made much of him because—they said—he was the most beautiful boy in the whole world.

And when it rained in Lavallette when she was growing up, she'd told him, they drove over to Tom's River to the library and she got a stack of books and brought them home and lay on the built-in bed on the screened-in porch and drank Pepsis and ate potato chips and read and read and read—

In Lavallette, she'd discovered buried treasure. Two men—Uncle Roy and Uncle Jim, who were really not her uncles—said they had found a map and a key. They told her and her brothers and her sister that the map said there was treasure on an island off the bay. They wondered if they all wanted to go find it. They took the map and they took a shovel and they walked to the bay—her sister and her two brothers—and Uncle Jim and Uncle Roy rowed them over to the island on the other side of the pier and they got out and they took out the map and they walked all around the island until they found the spot. The spot they found matched the X on the map, and they dug at that spot and sure enough, there was a treasure chest. A treasure chest as big as a small shoe box. It had leather straps and a lock. They opened it up with the key and it was full to overflowing with pennies. They took those and rowed back and walked to a place called the Cozy Nooke and sat down and called the waitress and told her all about the buried treasure and made her laugh and then they all had ice-cream cones and put the pennies side by side on top of the table and went outside and looked in the window to watch the waitress count them and they stood there and laughed until she had counted every one—

OH GEEZ, SHE'D SAY just out of nowhere when they were alone, *Lavallette!*

And then she would begin again. *Lavallette was like a dream, Riley.*

One night every summer, she said, they would drive over to the boardwalk at Seaside Heights. This boardwalk was not like the boardwalk in Lavallette. The boardwalk in Lavellette was for strolling and talking, for walking up and down for your exercise or your pleasure—like the Seawall in Galveston. There were little wooden pavilions on the boardwalk in Lavallette and her mother and her auntie—who always came for a week every year—would sit down there and talk. She would listen to them. Her mother told the same stories over and over again. She knew them so well that she could tell them herself, sort of the same way Riley knew her stories about Lavallette. They were his stories now, as if he'd grown up going to Lavallette himself.

He knew them so well he thought he might even start telling them to the tub men.

The boardwalk at Seaside Heights was very different from the boardwalk at Lavallette. It had two Ferris wheels and two merry-go-rounds, one each at either end of it. In between were fortune wheels and arcades with Skee-Ball games where you could win prizes like combs and jack sets. There were swami ladies in glass booths who for a nickel would slowly raise their plaster arms and try to pick up something from a pile of toys to give you—they mostly missed. And there was this haunted house and up above it was a big, huge, ugly woman whose face rocked back and forth and she would laugh really loud—*Ah HHHHHHAAAHHHA HA HA*, his mother would imitate her. She scared his mother and her brothers and sister to death. Somewhere near the haunted house and the lady with the loud laughing, there was a trailer, right in the middle of the boardwalk. *Ma always made us go inside.* You went up a set of stairs to get in the trailer, then you turned and walked alongside an iron lung with a huge window in it so you could see the body of the person inside. The body was covered with a blanket. Then you had to walk along to the top of the iron lung and around the person's head to get out. You had to look at that person's face and they had to look at you. Around that person's head was a little shelf where her mother made her put some of the nickels and dimes she really wanted to spend playing Skee-Ball.

Can you imagine my mother making us do that, Riley?—

Can you imagine they put people on display like that?

14

One afternoon between visiting hours, when Carnell Hughes was asleep and Melvin Pitts was down in the playroom and Parker MacGwyn was off somewhere with the physical therapist exercising his ankle, a lady named Marilyn Hooper came to visit Riley.

Marilyn Hooper told Riley that she was the hospital's psychiatrist and that she had already met his mother and father and she had heard a lot about Riley and had wanted to come meet him and had even stopped by to see him on many different occasions but that he'd often been asleep or the room had been full of company and so she had waited. She was glad he was by himself.

Marilyn Hooper told Riley that she knew all there was to know about fire because she and her whole family had been in one. Riley could see that was true because there was something about her arms and part of her face—the skin was ripply and many different colors—that made his stomach a little shaky.

Marilyn Hooper told Riley about looking out of the window of her house—which was up in the mountains in Nevada—and seeing the forest fire coming toward them in such a way that there was no escape. *I felt real scared,* Marilyn Hooper said. *I felt like I was going to die, except that my husband found a way for us to get out, one of us at a time. When our two sons got out, there was fire on their clothes and that made me really scared. There must have been fire on my clothes, too, but I didn't pay attention, I didn't care, because I was only worried about the boys. And then there was a neighbor driving by in his truck and he saw us and came and got us—*

Marilyn Hooper said that the easiest part of the whole fire to go through was getting out. Everything else was really hard: the hospital, the doctors, the nurses, the tubs, the physical therapy, going back home. *I cried whenever I saw the tub men coming,* Marilyn Hooper said.

Marilyn Hooper asked Riley how he felt about the tubs and he said they were okay and told her the joke about God's first name, though she didn't seem to get it either and said she'd have to get Jackson and Johnson to explain it to her and then she asked him if she could show him how to breathe when he saw the tub men coming. She made him shut his eyes and think about being in a place that made him really happy and right away without hardly thinking, he thought about being on the beach in Lavallette sitting next to his New Jersey grandmother—the one who always sent twenty-five dollars for his birthday and twenty-five dollars for Christmas—and his mother, with the water lapping up around his feet and the warm sun and sand all around him. And then Marilyn Hooper told him to get himself very comfortable in that happy spot and to keep it carefully in his mind and then to breathe very slowly, back and forth, back and forth.

Riley must have fallen asleep because the next thing he remembered was Marilyn Hooper saying, *So what about your fire, Riley? Do you want to talk about that?*

He shook his head—just a little. He was resting there on the beach in Lavallette with his mother and grandmother and wasn't ready yet to go anywhere else.

BUT THAT NIGHT, just before he fell asleep, Riley explained things to himself this way—and it all made perfect sense: A boy who'd spent his whole life being too big for his age—a boy named Riley Martin—was suddenly and without warning sent out on a journey. His adventures were the sort of thing that happened to Wonder Woman (every afternoon at five) or the Six Million Dollar Man (reruns at six).

He hadn't really intended to go anywhere. He was just

fine where he was in his house on Louisville Street in El Paso: okay mother, okay father, his own wonderful dog, a grandma off in Memphis who sent twenty dollars on his birthday, that second grandma in New Jersey who sent twenty-five, his best friend Greg up the block, a TV in the living room—a life that lacked nothing. Except, possibly, adventure—or otherwise, obviously, there would have been no need for him to go anywhere.

The signal for him to get up and start moving was a match. He lit it himself—he'd thought about it before, he just wanted to see what would happen, just a test, that sort of thing—and at that signal, the big boy—the one whose size everyone always seemed to have something to say about—as if he took up more than his share of space—Riley Martin—without intending to go anywhere (though maybe he really did), without really being prepared (he hadn't, for instance, told Greg)—set out on his journey.

This same thing had happened before, he pointed out to the nighttime audience of his imagination. Take, for instance, the spinning wheel of Sleeping Beauty. Sleeping Beauty, whose incredibly perfect story he had heard on his tape player at home many times, had also taken a journey. It was a clear-cut one, its course set at birth because her parents didn't want to invite the Bad Fairy to

Sleeping Beauty's christening. Because they couldn't put up with a little trouble and inconvenience—a weakness, he thought, similar to the one his own parents sometimes had—Sleeping Beauty had a destiny. That's what the tape called it. *A destiny*: at the age of sixteen, she would fall into a deep sleep from the prick of a needle on a spinning wheel.

Now. Here was the deal (Riley put out his hand flat to ward off any comments from his imaginary audience): no matter what Sleeping Beauty's parents did to prevent her from meeting her destiny, she was drawn to that needle like nobody's business. *There is no way to get around a destiny*—Riley narrowed his almost sleeping eyes and whispered out loud, sounding just like the cackling Bad Fairy on the tape. The emphasis on that remark was for his parents who, Riley was sure, probably didn't see things the way he did. He was sure they had tried to prevent his destiny just like Sleeping Beauty's parents had tried to prevent hers: told him a hundred times not to play with matches, told him a hundred times that fire was dangerous, kept matches and gasoline hidden away in the garage. But it hadn't done any good.

The fire had called him, just as sure a thing as the needle on Sleeping Beauty's spinning wheel—the match was lit and the journey began. Out he went, no questions asked, coming to Galveston by plane, arriving at the hospital in an ambulance—swollen, wrapped in bandages, carried high on a stretcher into the Acute Ward by two black men he had never seen before in his lifetime, the same black men who turned out to be his friends, the tub men, Jackson and Johnson.

And the hospital was a new country, as dark and foreign as any Treasure Island Jim Hawkins had ever sailed to, full of noises and crying like nothing he'd dreamed of before—a secret harbor of pain where his ship had surely dropped anchor. And because he was now one of its citizens, Riley, when he began to get better, explored every inch of it.

He knew the Acute Ward intimately, its fifteen beds—some full, some not. He knew every person who was there—when they came, how they'd gotten burned, how long they were going to stay, and when they left. A baby had died in Room 315 just the week before—her mother had put her in a tub of scalding water. While she was dying all the kids had to go down to the playroom and stay until the doctors had done everything they could—it gave him the willies just thinking about it.

He knew what the doctor said about each kid and what their parents were like—the mother of the boy in Room 317 took drugs—Parker's mother said so. That very day Mr. Loflin had told him about a new girl who they put right away in isolation. An airplane had crashed into her house and killed her best friend who was lying right next to her on the floor watching TV—the story was on the news all day. Her name was Rachel.

Riley didn't know the Reconstruction Ward—with its fifteen more beds and horrifying inhabitants in various stages of repair—as well as he knew the Acute Ward. This was mostly because the Reconstruction Ward was on the other side of the hospital, and Riley—from the Acute Ward—was a stranger there, an intruder of sorts, not comfortable walking around visiting like he did on the Acute Ward. The Reconstruction kids were mostly older than Riley and harder to know because they only came into the hospital for a week or two at a time to get work on old grafts or to get ears or fingers or noses.

The tub men told him all about it. When you came in for reconstruction, they said, the first day was surgery, then the next few days you laid in bed recovering. But just as soon as they could, the Reconstruction kids went down and played pool in the playroom and/or ran up and down the halls. *Ohhhhh, they full of energy!* the tub men said—Riley saw their heads flying past the windows of Room 312.

Sometimes he took the back way down to the playroom, which went along one side of the Reconstruction Ward, trying to stare in and see what he could see. If one of the kids there caught Riley's attention—and they always did—all he would have to do was ask the tub men or Mr. Loflin about them—mentioning the color of their skin or what body part was missing—and one or the other of those three men would cheerfully provide complete details.

Riley also knew all the rooms going down to the surgery room and then the surgery room itself—though he was usually half-asleep by the time he got there—and the playroom and the tub room on the first floor with its two joking—and sometimes frightening—attendants.

But his favorite place was the clinic on the second floor that on Tuesdays and Thursdays was filled with the most fascinating kids—all shapes and sizes and colors, bandaged and pinned together, missing arms and legs and noses, with contorted lips or strange outcroppings of skin—wounded soldiers in a complex battle, coming in twice a week for the sole purpose of fueling and confounding Riley's intense imagination. He wandered among them, staring at them as fully and unabashedly as if *he* were the doctor, and at night they fairly populated his dreams.

I am their hero!

Yes. In the daytime, Riley supposed it might appear—*to the naked eye*—that he was just a powerless ten-year-old—though he was really only seven—who wore a brown elastic hood over a white plastic mask that covered his face, who had his arms and legs wrapped in splints and ace bandages, who was totally under the control of his mother—who sat by his bed all day long—and at the mercy of his roommates.

But—*night was another thing*. At night his body knew no bounds. Parker and Melvin and Carnell had no idea where he went to—to their dim eyes and clouded minds it appeared that his too-big body just lay there in bed. But at night—ah!—at night his enemies were in peril of their lives.

For example: There were people in El Paso—sixth graders!—who always lounged around on the porch and steps of the house two doors down from his house, talking and laughing. They used to call out *Baby Baby Baby* when they saw Riley and laugh at him when he fell off his bike and cried and they used to make fun when he and Greg—his very best friend in all the world—skipped down the street holding hands.

But, at night, those same horrible boys came crawling up to Riley to bawl out their shame. *Forgive us*, they cried, putting their heads down on Riley's tennies, grabbing his ankles, black tears of sorrow and remorse spilling down their faces, snot pouring out of their noses and running into their mouths, slobbering. *Riley Riley Riley please forgive us*, they begged, *we didn't know you and Greg were such wonderful boys. Such big boys yourselves—not babies at all. Won't you play with us?*

Call me Riley *Martin*, he told those horrible sixth-grade boys in the midnight hours and he didn't give them an inch of compassion. Of course, he wouldn't play with them! And then he and Greg—but not Greg's cousin Jason—*heaven forbid!*—would single-handedly force those boys to sit down on the steps of their house and they would make them promise that they would never laugh at them ever again. *Ever!* And then they would make those horrible, lazy boys—sweep the sidewalk!—so that Greg and Riley could skip down it without ever falling on a rock and ride their bikes and it would all be smooth sailing.

At night Greg was there with Riley in his dreams, his loyal henchman—the Tonto to his Lone Ranger, the Robin to his Batman—and together they took over the universe.

One glorious night, in fact, Riley ripped off his clothes—just like Superman—to save everyone in the clinic and the hospital from a hurricane. The storm was coming in from the ocean, tearing off the tops of the palm trees, slamming against the plate-glass windows, howling and crying down through every room. It had been on the news all day. Greg held Riley's ace bandages and rubber face mask and elastic hood while he, golden horns spouting from the top of his head, cape aflutter, shattered the eye of the storm with one blow of his blazing ax. The little kids on the Acute Ward and the older boys and girls in Reconstruction, sometimes haughty toward Riley in the day—not even paying attention to him when he asked to play pool—especially when he was with Melvin—they seemed to have something against him—and he knew they didn't like Melvin—spoke of his deeds all up and down the nighttime halls.

Avast ye hearties, they whispered through their bandages, *have you heard about our matey, Riley?* And Parker MacGwyn ordered the doctors to have an ice-cream party in the playroom so everyone could clap and sing to Riley. They lined up to shake his hand AND they cheered like crazy when he walked in the room AND they laid down their pool sticks at his feet.

Another night, Riley banished Melvin Pitts to the outer limits beyond the world of Room 312. His very best friend Greg, who had never met Melvin Pitts in real life, held the door open so he, Riley, could boot Melvin out of the hospital forever. Parker MacGwyn called in the tub men and the nurses—sweeping his hand around the room to show them how Riley had cleaned out all its disturbing elements—and handed over control of the remote to Riley.

15

Riley missed his father all the time. He waited for the weekends when his dad could fly to Galveston from El Paso, waited to hear the sound of his father's laugh, to see him get so tickled about something he'd double over or fall nearly backward out of his chair, to study his father's face as it wrinkled and twisted when he talked, to smell that particular smell of cigarettes and coffee and—sometimes—onions that was his father's very own way of smelling.

Riley liked Parker's father, Kingsley—the only other man he knew at the hospital except Dr. Walker and Mr. Loflin and Jackson and Johnson and Gene—but Kingsley MacGwyn had never stood in the middle of the room and read *Alice in Wonderland* out loud all one Saturday afternoon like Lewis Martin had—the sound of his voice almost making Riley want to cry. Kingsley MacGwyn had never bought comic books for each boy in the room, nor gone to Colonel Bubbie's Army/Navy Surplus Store and bought hiking shorts with flapped-over pockets and filled the pockets full of Starbursts and M&Ms and fishing flies and pocketknives and sat surrounded by the boys in the room with Carnell Hughes on his lap and Melvin Pitts sputtering in his ear, while he talked about moose and alligators and snakes and the best way to sleep out in pup tents. Kingsley had never sung *Christmas is a-coming, the geese are getting fat, won't you please to put a penny in an old man's hat* while he did a jig all around the room with his long, bony legs knuckling back and forth, and Kingsley had never suddenly and without warning fallen down flat on the floor just for the heck of it and just to see the surprise on Riley's face.

No, Kingsley MacGwyn was all business and Bermuda shorts and jingling the change in his pockets and paying attention to his wife and mostly talking just to her and to Parker and Riley's mother and sometimes to Riley, with an occasional *Hey fella* to Carnell and Melvin. But Riley's dad was not like that. When he came to visit, everybody was excited.

Except maybe Riley's mother. It was Riley's mother who acted funny when his dad was around even though she was always telling Parker's mother about him and about his wonderful job and about how much she missed him and what a great husband and father he was.

But when Riley's father actually arrived on those much-too-short weekends, it was a different story. When his mother and father and Riley were finally alone in the room, his mother would sit in the chair beside Riley's bed with her arms folded up over her chest and her purse on her lap, as if she had no intention of making herself comfortable—even though on most days she put her purse in Riley's nightstand as soon as she came in the room. Out of nowhere, she would sigh loud enough for both Riley and his father to hear.

What's the matter? Riley's father would say.

You need to chew some gum, Lewis, she would say to him.

Why? Does my breath stink?

Smell, she corrected him.

Does my breath smell? he wanted to know.

Well, we did just eat onions, she said. And you didn't brush your teeth. And it's not like we're the only people in the room, you know, she said, pursing her lips. She gave him some gum.

Not ten minutes later, she would sigh again. He was chewing too loud and with his mouth open—why did he have to crack his gum, she didn't crack hers—and—she added—you have dandruff. She flicked at the back of his shoulders with her hand. Why don't you use a dandruff shampoo? She would push and poke like that until Riley's father would suddenly scream *Shit!*

And then tears would break out in her eyes—and Riley's, too—and his father would say he just couldn't stand it, he just couldn't, when she would talk to him like that. Then she would say she was sorry, she was really sorry, she was just going crazy and she missed him and she had no one to talk to except Corliss MacGwyn and Corliss was no help at all and then he would say he was sorry, too, and she would cry for a while and then she would say she had to go to the bathroom and she would get up and go out of the room. And then Riley's father would tell him that his mother was having a really hard time with all this, the fire, and staying at the hospital all by herself and everything that was going on, she was taking it all very hard, and that made it so she cried a lot and then he would remind Riley to please take care of his mother and then he would sit there on the edge of Riley's bed and work his tongue around in his mouth until Riley's mother came back in the room and then she would put her purse away in Riley's nightstand and sit down and make a funny face at her husband and then he would grab the edge of her knee and squeeze it until she said, No, don't, stop, that tickles, and then she would brighten up a little. At least until Parker's mother and father showed up and then she would frown again while Lewis made a fool of himself—as she put it later when the room was empty—in front of them.

I hate rich Southerners, his father would say. *That's why we left Memphis, remember?*

You don't have to sit in the same room with them all day, his mother would shoot back. *I can't be rude.*

Whenever Riley's father came, he brought word from Greg—Riley's best friend in all the world—and pictures: one of their dog, Lady Luck, and different ones that each of the neighbors had sent along. He brought stories about what was going on at home and how Riley's first-grade teacher, Mrs. Althoff, was always calling and asking about him.

She really misses you, Riley. We all do.

What did you tell her, Dad? Riley wanted to know. Did you tell her about the hospital? And about Melvin and Parker and Carnell Hughes and Room 312? Does she know about the tub men and all the jokes they tell and how they sing? Did you tell her about surgery? Say, Dad, do you know why they have such big lamps in the surgery room? And is Lady Luck still digging holes in the backyard?

But the news about Lady Luck on Lewis Martin's last visit had not been so good. Little Lady Luck—the scroungy pup they'd just months before gotten from the pound, the one that all the kids in the neighborhood came to the door asking to have a peek at, the one that Bertha next door wanted her big dog Turko to marry as soon as Lady Luck was old enough—had died. Neglect, sorrow, despair, confusion—Riley's father didn't know the exact medical reason, he said, but he told Riley he was sure it was because her heart was broken when Riley left, and no amount of explaining that he'd be back could cure her.

16

Riley thought about his best friend Greg almost all the time. There were no other boys in the whole world like Greg. Greg liked TV and puzzles and listening to tapes and reading books just like Riley did. Greg and Riley had played together every day since the day they first met each other when they were only three and every day in the summer in the hot afternoons they played in the big plastic pool in Riley's backyard and they talked about things, about this and that, and they would not let Sarah, the six-year-old redheaded girl who lived across the street who was in love with both of them, get in the pool with them at the same time and when she tried to climb in the car with them if they were going somewhere, they made her sit in the back while the two of them squeezed up together in the front seat.

One thing Riley knew for sure—he had to get home as fast as he could because his being gone had to be tearing Greg apart. He knew this because Greg had sent a letter that said:

I hope you are getting better. I am doing fine. I got your letter from you. I understand that you are my best friend. Me and Sarah and Jason have been playing after school. Do you know when you are coming back? That's all. Greg.

Sarah! Jason!

One day Greg called. It had been a bad day for Riley. The tub men had come when he was hungry and he had had to go to the bathroom and the tub men and their picking and scraping where his skin was still open had hurt so much, he peed right in the water—again!—which made the two old tub men laugh—also again. *Whoooeee*, boy, they hooted. *We're getting so's we can depend on you!* But Riley didn't think it was very funny. It made him mad that they had made him pee and acted like he peed all the time—he'd only peed one other time—or maybe two—and he stewed about it as he lay in his bed after the bath.

Right then the nurse brought the telephone into the room, as if Greg—with the extrasensory powers of friendship—had known just what kind of a day Riley was having.

It's a friend of yours named Greg, she told him.

Oh, it's Greg, said Riley. He took the phone. Listen, Greg, said Riley, getting right to the point, who have you been playing with? Have you been playing with Jason? What about Sarah?

Jason? Not too much. Just a little after school. Sarah? In the afternoons.

Who do you walk home with? Jason and Sarah?

Yeah.

The conversation went on just a little longer. Greg said he was sorry about Lady Luck, but Riley couldn't pay attention after he heard about Jason and Sarah from Greg's own mouth. That was bad news. Jason, Greg's eight-year-old cousin who lived on the next block over, had been horning in on Greg and Riley's friendship for a long time and there wasn't really anything at all that Riley could do about it. You can't, after all, complain about a cousin. A cousin is like part of the furniture. You could tell a regular person to go away, you could complain about a regular person—but a cousin? Never! You'd get in trouble with everybody if you tried to say something about a cousin.

It was a horrible situation. And Sarah—a girl—another problem entirely—was always trying to break them apart, too. Now that Riley was gone, it looked like the two of them were succeeding. Even if Jason wasn't his cousin and Sarah wasn't a girl, Greg would never tell them to go away. Greg was like that. He didn't see that being best friends with someone meant that you couldn't be friends with anyone else.

But that wasn't how Riley saw it. When you had a best friend, you didn't need other friends. You only needed your best friend. Other friends just complicated things. A best friend was the person you told everything to. A best friend was someone who called you on the telephone before you called him and wanted you to come to his house and eat dinner and you were the only one invited. A best friend always had only you on his mind, like you always only had him on your mind.

But Greg had other friends because everybody liked Greg. He had blond hair that stuck up in the back of his head and he had a very nice way of saying Riley Martin instead of just Riley when he wanted Riley's attention and he had a smile that made his whole face bright—Riley couldn't think of Greg without seeing light spreading out all around his head.

Greg wasn't a big boy like Riley was a big boy. Greg wasn't too tall and he wasn't too fat. He was just right—a boy who was seven who looked like he was seven. But Greg was a seven-year-old boy who understood the difficulties that boys who were seven who looked like they were ten went through because Riley had told him and Greg understood.

Greg didn't talk too much. He let other boys boss him around and never minded at all. Everybody liked him because he was so easy. Greg was so easy he would just let Sarah come play with him. Greg was so easy he might even agree with Jason if Jason wanted to be not just his cousin, but his best friend. Greg might tell Sarah he would marry her. Just the thought cut Riley to the quick. He wanted to be home really bad so he and Greg could play together and so he could make sure Greg was his best friend.

His heart ached. He longed to talk to someone, to have a best friend right here at the hospital. A temporary best friend would do, just someone to help him through the long days. The person he ended up with most was Carnell Hughes. No matter where Riley went, Carnell was there with him, smiling a little tiny trembly grin even when Riley wasn't very nice. Somehow Carnell's sweetness bothered Riley more than anything. If Riley wanted to go to the bathroom, Carnell followed, standing shivering outside the door until Riley was finished—Carnell was always cold. Every time Riley thought he might sneak to the playroom, Carnell limped right along behind him.

And Carnell Hughes was okay, but he didn't really count as a friend, let alone a best friend, because Carnell Hughes was only four and Riley was seven.

The best friend he thought would be right—at the hospital, that is—was Parker MacGwyn. Riley admired Parker MacGwyn because he was a teenager and nothing ever seemed to bother him, not even Melvin Pitts. Parker just sat in the chair next to his bed in the blue-striped pajamas his mother had brought him from home, the remote control in his hand, changing the channels whenever he liked, no matter what Melvin Pitts cried about. Nothing fazed Parker. He said *Yes ma'am* and *Yes sir* to everyone and all the nurses and even the tub men liked him and said he was a gentleman. Parker got all the presents he wanted because his mother and father and his uncles and aunts and grandparents were rich and brought or sent him presents every day. Louisiana, after all, was not very far away from Galveston, so he had plenty of visitors. Parker even got autographed photos from movie stars.

But the thing that attracted Riley the most was that Parker didn't seem to need a friend, let alone a best friend—at least not the way Riley did. Parker was perfectly content to be by himself, as if his own companionship was completely satisfying.

He was his own best friend.

17

One afternoon Riley asked Parker how his ankle got burned. For the first and only time, Riley saw Parker get upset. His face turned red. He even turned the TV off so everyone could hear what he had to say.

I have NO IDEA how it happened, he said, staring hard at Riley. I was asleep, he said. One of my friends was drinking. *I don't drink!* Parker declared before anyone else in the room could say a word and by that time Carnell and Melvin were listening, too.

Another one of Parker's friends had cigarettes.

Not me! Parker said, as if someone was accusing him. Parker wasn't even in the same room with these friends at some girl's house when her parents were gone for the weekend. He was waiting outside for a ride from . . . somebody who would give him one because it was past eleven and he *knew* his mother and father wanted him to be home before curfew and he *knew* they wouldn't like him to be at this girl's house when her parents weren't home. He must have fallen asleep and then earlier when those friends of his were drinking there at this girl's house—he tried to tell them not to go to her house since her parents weren't there, but they had the car and he couldn't just get out and walk, could he?—one of them must have poured some gin on his ankle and it didn't dry and then later when he was outside sleeping waiting for the ride, some one of them must have thrown a cigarette out and it landed on his ankle. But he had no idea who could have done it. In fact, he didn't really know any of the people who were at that girl's house that night. He'd never seen any of them before.

Oh, anybody can see you were drinking, Parker, Melvin Pitts howled. You're lying. You were just drunk and you set yourself on fire.

Shut up, Melvin! Parker shot back.

Dr. Walker said that the burn on *your* ankle is the *worst* burn he's ever seen—*I heard him*. You must have drunk a whole bottle of gin yourself and it came leaking out of your body and you just caught on fire because you were so full of alcohol, that's what happened!

Was you drunk, Parker MacGwyn? Carnell Hughes chimed in.

He wasn't drunk! Riley declared earnestly, even though

he'd heard his mother say that Parker *was* drunk. But Parker wouldn't lie! Riley was sorry he had asked Parker about his ankle. It had upset Parker and now everybody in the room was asking him questions.

But Parker had had enough. He turned the TV back on to show that he was finished talking about how his ankle got burned and clicked the channels around until he came to a show *he* wanted to watch, a rerun of *Superman II*.

Clark Kent and Lois Lane were together in a honeymoon suite where they had been assigned to pose as newlyweds to expose the inflated prices of the hotel.

Oh, I don't want to watch *Superman* again, Melvin complained. I've seen it a hundred times. And it's not even the beginning.

You can't even count to a hundred, Melvin, said Parker. So shut up. And if you've seen it a hundred times, you don't need to start at the beginning.

I love *Superman*, said Riley.

Oh, you love everything Parker loves, Liar, Melvin Pitts said.

Lois Lane was disgusted with Clark's bumbling ways. She suspected that he was keeping his real identity from her. Earlier that day she had tried to trick him by throwing herself into Niagara Falls to see if he would turn into

Superman and save her, but he—able to see her motives—saved her instead by cutting a branch above her head with his X-ray vision so that she could hold onto it and save herself. Riley, having also seen the movie nearly a hundred times, was overcome once more at Superman's narrow escape.

Now came the part that Riley hated: In the honeymoon suite, Lois asked Clark to bring her hairbrush over by the circular fire where she was sitting but Clark tripped. His glasses fell into the fire. He plunged his hand in after them and fumbled to put them back on. Lois Lane grabbed his hand and stared at it—it hadn't even been burned!

If only Clark hadn't dropped his glasses, Riley always fretted at this point in the movie. He saw it as the beginning of the end—a tiny mistake that led to a terrible and tragic fall, an awful turning away from Superman's true purpose. He hated the thought that Lois Lane had found out Superman's secret. He blamed the rest of the movie on her.

Oh boy, said Melvin Pitts, now for the *real* fun.

Parker laughed a strange laugh, as if he was agreeing with Melvin. That confused Riley. Didn't Parker understand that Superman was about to lose all his power? How could Parker laugh at a time like this?

Lois Lane tried to hold onto Clark Kent's hand, but he got up and walked away. He stood with his back to her, trying to make up his mind if he should walk out of the room or kiss her—*oh, terrible fate*—because if he kissed her, he could never be Superman again!

Go for it, baby, yelled Melvin Pitts. Peaches and cream. Jello.

Um um, said Parker without moving his lips. The sound came from deep down inside him.

Riley Martin held his breath and chewed on the ace bandage that covered his hand.

Clark Kent straightened his shoulders. His decision was made. He turned, took off his glasses, and looked at Lois, his eyes suddenly watery.

Oh no, said Riley, he's going to lose his identity.

Yeah, boy, hooted Melvin.

Clark and Lois kissed.

I never would have done that, said Riley with disappointment, for the hundredth time.

You never will either, yelled Melvin.

Parker MacGywn looked over at Riley then and rolled his eyes, but Riley wasn't sure what he meant by that.

18

Every Sunday afternoon at four there was a Bible Club in the playroom. The Sunday School lady gave prizes of all sorts—prizes for attendance, prizes for the person who was the quietest, and big prizes for memorizing verses.

The verse they were supposed to have ready that week was John 10:9 and the prize was a miniature Rubik's cube that glowed in the dark with scenes from Jesus' life.

John 9:10, John 9:10, Carnell kept saying over and over. I the door.

John 10:9, Riley corrected. I *am* the door.

Paint me green and yellow, Melvin Pitts yelled.

No, no, Melvin, said Riley. He frowned. These are the words of Jesus.

John 10, said Carnell Hughes, his thin-lipped smile quivering. He punched the paper with the verses from the week before and mumbled to himself in imitation of Riley.

John 6: Bread of life. John 9: Door. You better say you verse, Melvin Pitts.

Oh shut up, dummy, Melvin Pitts sputtered. You can't even read, you dummy. And who wants a stupid Rubik's cube anyway?

The nurse came to tell them the club was starting.

Melvin was out the door in a flash. Parker's mother, her perfume preceding, her high heels clicking on the floor, pushed Parker down the hallway. Riley followed closely after, with Carnell Hughes wobbling along behind him like a drunk and his own mother walking close to the wall and staring at the floor. John 8:12, Riley repeated to himself solemnly, I am the light of the world.

THAT WAS THE DAY, Riley remembered, when he first saw Pat, the meanest girl in the whole world, who LaKeesha had whispered to him about when he first came to the hospital.

That was also the day that Mr. Loflin came screeching and banging into Room 312 first thing in the morning with the news that Pat—that same Pat—had finally got what she'd been crying about: *Uncle Jimmy's done up and come. Hallelujah!*

Uncle Jimmy? Carnell had piped up, though it was to Parker MacGwyn that Mr. Loflin generally directed his news about Pat and the other patients at the hospital, and it was Miss MacGwyn who always provided the *Bless-his-heart* commentary on whatever godforsaken creature was being discussed—in addition to more than enough advice should that person consider mending his or her way.

That's right, Parker, Mr. Loflin had said, popping his chewing gum. Uncle Jimmy's here. That gal Hattie with the jingle-jangle earrings is gone. Finally wore out her welcome. Said she was Pat's mother but didn't act like no mother. Don't ask me to name what she acted like, and excuse me for saying so right in front of you, Miss MacGwyn. All she cared about was staying at the Holiday Inn *with the king siiize TVs*. Leastways that's what she said.

Miss MacGwyn had groaned in preparation for her lecture, but Mr. Loflin had started fussing and straightening and fiddling around, just the way he did every morning, getting everybody all stirred up, filling up the room with all his noise and bustle. And he kept right on talking.

That old Pat thinks she's the queen now that Uncle Jimmy's here, is what Mr. Loflin had said. She said he done killed a man, said he's going to kill all of us, said she told him to because we been so mean to her. HA HA

HA! Wants us to feed her every bite, wants us to carry her to the bathroom, says her feet hurt, says we better do it or Uncle Jimmy's going to kill us. But she don't spit her food out and she don't pee in her bed now that Uncle Jimmy's here. No sireee! Uncle Jimmy's gonna straighten that old gal out! *Yessireebob!*

Who killed who? Melvin had wanted to know.

Hush, Melvin! Parker's mother had said.

Uncle Jimmy killed a man! Mr. Loflin screeched. Didn't you hear me?

What man?

How the hell do I know? You think I know everything? You think I'm going to ask Uncle Jimmy who he up and killed?

That was the day that Miss MacGwyn had very much to say about—*Bless their hearts*—black people and the *terrible* way they conducted themselves, all of which she declared in a loud voice for everyone to hear, including Carnell Hughes, who listened as cheerfully as if he were white. During Miss MacGwyn's recital, Riley's mother didn't say a word—only sat in her chair with her arms folded up over her chest. She got up in the middle of one of Miss MacGwyn's sentences and went to the bathroom, shutting the door behind her a lot louder than usual.

IT TURNED OUT THAT LaKeesha was right—Pat didn't look like a girl at all, or like a boy either, but only like a chalky, pale thing who sat in a chair all wrapped in blankets and trembled and shook and cried out every few minutes in the most strangled, tinny voice that sounded like it had somehow gotten stuck in the back of her throat, *Can't somebody help me? Can't somebody help me?* But nobody paid any attention to her—not even the Sunday School teacher or the playroom lady—except the thin black man who sat next to her, who everybody from Room 312 knew for sure had to be *Uncle Jimmy*. He told Pat to shut up.

That was the same day that Melvin yelled right away, *Did you really kill a man?* at Pat's Uncle Jimmy and got Pat to hollering and screaming so loud that Mr. Loflin had to come in and fuss at her, and that was the same day that Riley's mother made the mistake of saying hello to Pat and telling Pat who she was and Pat told Riley's mother she was ugly and had bad breath and then right away tried to tell her everything about how she got to the hospital but she talked so fast and her voice shook so much, Riley's mother couldn't understand her at all.

You talking too fast, girl, her uncle Jimmy had told her. She don't understand a word you saying.

And then Uncle Jimmy fleshed out the story himself.

Pat was mad at Hattie, he said. *Hattie wouldn't give Pat no ice and Pat didn't like Hattie's boyfriend*, he said real slow. *So Pat poured gasoline on the barbecue and lit a match.*

Ohhh, his mother had said. Well. How long have you been here, Pat?

Ever since the fire, Pat cried out.

That was the very day that Pat must have decided that she was going to do everything she could to get herself moved to Room 312 so she could be near Riley's mother. That was the way Pat was, Riley came to find out too late. She hated the people she loved. Or maybe she loved the people she hated. Riley couldn't figure out which.

That was also the day that the Sunday School teacher told them how Jesus had waited until Lazarus was completely dead to go to his house even though everyone—including Riley—wondered why and thought maybe Jesus wasn't very nice and how Lazarus' sisters, Mary and Martha, had come running out to ask him where have you been? And that Lazarus was already dead by then and Mary said he stinketh but how Jesus wasn't the least bit worried because he knew what was going to happen next and what happened next was that Jesus stood outside of the place where Lazarus was buried and everyone waited to see what he would do.

And right here, the Sunday School lady, an old lady with white hair and glasses who always talked so quiet you could hardly hear her, raised her arms and fluttered them up and down and yelled, *Lazarus, come forth*—in a voice like an old crow. And Lazarus, the old teacher said—her voice trembling with tears—with white rags wound all around him and a cloth covering his face and walking dazed and battered like someone who had been in a terrible fight, came out of the cave and he wasn't dead at all even though he had been once and if it hadn't been for Jesus he would still be dead. And Jesus said to everybody standing around, Take off the grave clothes and let him go.

That was the same day that Melvin Pitts kept going on and on about Uncle Jimmy and kept fidgeting and finally sat on the sofa on his knees and when the Sunday School lady yelled at Lazarus to come forth, Melvin laughed so loud he tried to stand up without realizing where his feet were and fell off the sofa onto the floor and then stopped laughing and screamed and cried just like a big baby and Riley saw—really *saw* for the first time—what a big, overgrown boy looked like to other people and wished that he wasn't one himself and wished that he was like Greg—a boy who was seven who looked like he was seven. It made him feel so desperate, like he always did just before he went to surgery. And that—and the fact that Pat hadn't quit calling out, *Can't somebody help me?* in such a strange, horrible voice, and also the fact that he was in the room with a known murderer—all began to affect him so much that when the teacher asked if there was anyone who wanted Jesus to come into their heart and save them, Riley raised his hand. The teacher asked everyone who had raised their hand to come after class to talk to her and then Melvin—who hadn't raised his hand at all—followed Riley and the teacher to the back of the playroom and when the teacher asked the boys why they had raised their hands and Riley said it was because he wanted to ask Jesus into his heart, Melvin interrupted and said it was because he—Melvin—wanted a Rubik's cube and when the teacher told Melvin he couldn't have one until he memorized his verse, Melvin started crying and calling her a liar and then ran screaming down the hall to report her to the nurses.

19

One afternoon right after lunch, Parker's mother brought a man to Room 312. Parker's mother introduced him to Riley and to Riley's mother, but not to Melvin Pitts or to Carnell Hughes, who was taking his afternoon nap. The man's name was Father something.

He had black hair and shiny shoes. All his clothes were black except for the collar of his shirt, which was white. He had on perfume. It was on the bandages that wrapped Riley's hands and filling up the air in Room 312 all afternoon. Miss MacGwyn was talking and talking and telling this man all about the church she went to back in Louisiana. *St Jooohn's*, she said. And all about her Bible reading and her prayer groups and her prayer chains and her prayer lists and how she herself was a Daughter of the King. She gave him a big smile. Please call me Corliss, she told him. And would he please *a-noint* Parker, was how she said it, drawing it out and fluttering her eyelashes and the man smiled back at her and his face turned red.

Riley's mother squeezed her eyes shut for a minute, then opened them wide. Riley could see that she had clamped down on her cheeks inside her mouth—they were all pinched in—something she always did when she was upset. She didn't move. She just stared as the man took out a little brown bottle and tipped it over once between his fingers and touched Parker's head and mumbled some things that Riley couldn't hear while Parker's mother kept her eyes closed and held her lips together and twisted the ankle of her leg round and round.

Just before he left, the man looked over at Riley's mother. The minute he did that, she started to cry and she stood up then and went to him—there in the middle of the room and in front of everyone. And she told him how Riley was her son, her only son, her only child—she had wanted more, and she and her husband had tried, but nothing had happened—and how Riley had been the joy of her life. He was one of those boys that everyone stopped to look at when they saw him—tall for his age, strong, a natural leader with auburn hair the color of her own that waved just like his father's. He was big like his father and his heart was delicate and sensitive like his father's—*swollen with tears or crazy laughter like his father's*—but he also favored her own family, her own brothers who were talkers and hungry and voracious readers and were very serious about everything.

His mother laughed a little laugh that sounded like she was going to choke.

Why, Riley had wanted to read so badly just as soon as he first saw someone else do it—why, when he was very little, he would hold a book in his hand and babble along, turning the pages and holding the book upside down—oh, he was just such a wonderful boy!

I'm sure he's still a wonderful boy, the man said, his eyebrows pinched together.

Riley's mother ignored the man. *And now look at him—*

And everyone in the room had turned to look at Riley.

His mother said she couldn't understand why he—why he—she just didn't know why—she started crying again—maybe if she had gone to church the day of the fire—she'd started going back just recently—maybe then—but she hadn't gone that day—

Do you think that God is punishing you? the man asked her.

His mother frowned like she couldn't figure out what he'd said. She had no idea what God was doing, she told him, she only wanted to know what *she* was going to do.

Her husband wasn't here to help her. They could only afford for him to come every other weekend.

Then she got up really close to the man. *I want to know if you can heal Riley, can fix his face,* she said. And then she said really loud that it was Riley who needed healing more than ANYONE ELSE in the whole room or in the whole hospital, as a matter of fact. And she looked over at Parker's mother.

Riley wished she hadn't told the man so much and he wished she hadn't said it in front of everyone in Room 312, especially in front of Parker MacGwyn and his mother.

The man said hardly a word to Riley's mother after that, only turned in a businesslike way and put his hands on Riley's hands—or rather on top of the ace bandages which covered Riley's hands—and said, Let us pray, and then rubbed around in the air near Riley's head and then went over and said good-bye to Parker and his mother again—*Why, we're just so thrilled you came,* Miss MacGwyn said—and then left without once looking again at Riley or his mother.

Miss MacGywn didn't talk to his mother for the rest of the afternoon and when *Wonder Woman* came on at five—two hours before visiting time was over—she got up and did something she'd never done before: she left.

20

I want someone to be my friend, Melvin Pitts would bawl out every single day, lying face down on his bed and screaming *momma momma mommmaaaaa*, just like he was going to die. His demands for friendship were terrible.

I be your friend, Melvin Pitts, Carnell Hughes would tell him.

Not you, Carnell, Melvin Pitts would spit. Anybody but you. You're a nigger!

Nobody wants to be your friend, Melvin Pitts, Parker MacGwyn would say, switching the channels on the TV.

To have a friend, you must be a friend, Parker's mother would recite primly, brushing a piece of hair off the shoulder of her fluffy yellow sweater. You ought to know that, *Mister* Pitts.

The only thing I know, Melvin would cry, is that I want a friend. *Somebody* has to be my friend!

In his heart—with much fear and trembling—Riley felt that the *somebody* was supposed to be him. Melvin wouldn't let Carnell Hughes be his friend and Parker would never even consider Melvin—Parker was too good, too much better, to even waste his time talking to Melvin. That left only one person in the room who was eligible or capable of being the friend of Melvin Pitts and no excuse at all would do, Riley knew, because he'd tested all of them on his heart and none would pass:

- He already had a best friend—Greg.
- He didn't like Melvin Pitts.
- Melvin Pitts smelled like strawberry milk.
- If he was friends with Melvin Pitts, Parker MacGwyn would never talk to him again.

If Riley wouldn't be a friend to Melvin, Melvin wouldn't have a friend in the whole world. Because of his current separation from Greg and the possibility that Jason and Sarah had stolen Greg away, Riley felt deeply the terrifying consequences of being friendless. It was awful! He knew because Jason and Sarah had stolen Greg away once before and it had nearly killed him. It was one Saturday when Riley's mother had told him he couldn't go out and play because he hadn't cleaned up his room. But he had. He thought he had. He had tried cleaning it.

It looked fine. Anyway, there he was stuck inside pushing things under his bed and moping around, when he happened to look out the front window and there was Greg running down Louisville Street with Jason and Sarah and looking like he was having so much fun—almost *more fun* than Riley had ever seen him have before.

Riley was undone! Hadn't he already called Greg and told him he wouldn't be able to play that day? Hadn't Greg understood that he should tell everyone he couldn't play because Riley had to stay home? Hadn't Greg understood that he should tell Jason and Sarah just to go away?

Nobody deserved to be alone! When Riley pitted that outer darkness against all the above-mentioned not-so-good excuses for not being Melvin's best friend, along with the admonitions of the Sunday School teacher and his father—who he missed so much—to be kind . . . he didn't need strawberry milk to make his stomach churn.

He tested the possibilities of friendship with Melvin in case he should ever get the courage to cross the line. He tried out the first words he would say, but only in his mind: *Melvin, do you want to play?*

But no sooner were those words out of his mind's mouth than he saw Melvin pushing his bed up next to his own, chaining them together, yelling out all sorts of unmentionable things in that raspy, obnoxious, bad-breath-smelling voice of his, going around telling everyone that he and Riley were best friends. Parker would hate Riley for allowing that to happen. He would never talk to him again.

Riley's heart was very weak—he knew that only too well.

Somebody has to be my friend, Melvin would yell out again.

Riley's conscience ached. He tried once more—also in his mind. *Melvin!* (It might help to be firm). *Do you want to play?* But no sooner did he utter this more determined invitation then it was followed by a flood of ugly finger-shaking things Melvin would have to do before Riley would ever consider playing with him: *You must stop yelling you have to be nice you can't scream you have to talk quietly please don't stand so close to me please don't crash down on your bed please don't spit please don't say ugly words please don't laugh at what Jesus says I can't stand the way you smell like strawberry milk please don't fart!*

It was exhausting to think about all the things Melvin would have to change before he could possibly be Riley's friend.

21

A terrible boy with the face of a monster appeared in the playroom one day. Melvin Pitts let out a screechy wail when he first saw him and the sight of that boy's face took the breath right out of Riley Martin. Parker and Carnell could only stare at him—he had a shiny mass of bumpy skin pulled tight across his bones like a dead man's. He had eyes without eyebrows and flat lips and a nose that was, it seemed, only half a nose. He had no ears. His hands were like fat lumps, the fingers all swollen and spread out.

The boy had never before been seen anywhere by anyone. Then suddenly he was there, standing in the middle of the playroom with a pool cue resting on his awful hand like he was waiting for someone to play a game with him. Not one of the residents of Room 312 dared to talk to him and the desire to play pool—their main purpose in coming to the playroom in the first place—was sucked right out of them at the sight of him.

They would have stood and stared all day except that the playroom lady came in and got them all sorted out—Melvin Pitts and Parker with some video games, Riley with a classroom assignment he needed to work on, Carnell Hughes with a coloring book and some crayons.

Parker MacGwyn found out the next morning from the tub men that the monster boy was named Eddie Rabedeaux and that he was from New Orleans and that he had been electrocuted. A bolt of lightning had shot right through him, burned him from the inside out, the tub men told Parker. Yes sir, they said, boy in the wrong place at the wrong time, should have been home instead of wandering round during a storm. It ain't like you been, Paaarker, they said. You're burned on your skin. You're burned on the outside. Now, when you get electrocuted, everything melts on the inside, including your bones—that's why that boy's face look so terrible.

The four roommates, usually at such odds, were one in their fascination with Eddie. At every opportunity, Parker went over the information that the tub men had given him—neglecting to say, or forgetting to say, or not remembering to say that the tub men had also told him that Eddie was a regular gentleman. That being set aside,

Parker added freely to the story: Eddie was a very bad person from a very bad neighborhood and he was always getting into trouble and therefore—a natural conclusion—he'd been electrocuted. The four boys speculated on what terrible things he could have done to deserve such an awful punishment: robbed and stolen, talked back to his mother, killed his father, tortured other kids in the neighborhood, swore, never went to school, tied a little kid up in a bag and threw him in the dump. Been a bully. Said mean things to little kids. Tried to do things to a girl.

What girl would look at him? Melvin sputtered out suddenly. God, his face makes me sick. It makes my stomach sick!—it looks just like your face, Riley!

All three boys—Melvin, Parker, and Carnell—turned to look at Riley then.

Riley don't look like Eddie, said Carnell after a while.

Yes, he does, said Melvin Pitts. Riley's nose is just like Eddie's. It's all burned out!

He don't look like Eddie, repeated Carnell Hughes cheerfully. Eddie look all melted, Riley look all red. Ain't you seen yourself, Riley?

How can he see himself? screamed Melvin Pitts. There's not a mirror in the whole damn hospital!

Riley's okay, said Parker.

• • •

THE ROOMMATES LOOKED FOR Eddie everywhere, sneaking back along the hall to the playroom from every direction—up along the front of the hospital, down through the back. They checked out the clinic on the second floor. Melvin even got on the elevator pushing Parker in his chair so they could take a quick look in the lobby, but Eddie Rabedeaux had vanished.

The tub men told Parker the next day that Eddie had had surgery on his neck the afternoon before and if they wanted to find him they should look in one of the private rooms on the Reconstruction Ward. They probably wouldn't keep him in the wards with the other kids because he scared everybody. Except them, of course, the tub men said, because they were used to him. And also because Eddie was a regular gentleman. Ain't many like him, they said, though Parker didn't pay any attention again to that critical piece of information.

Two days after the first sighting of Eddie, Melvin reported that he'd seen him in one of the private rooms on the back hall of the Reconstruction Ward—he was sure it was him because the room was dark and his bed was turned so you couldn't see his face and he knew the doctors would want to keep that guy hidden away so nobody at all would have to look at him. He said Eddie was even scarier-looking than usual because they had him flat on his back with a wedge under his head so his neck would stay stretched out. Through the Venetian blinds covering his window, all you could see was the top of his head. What you could see of his face—already awful—looked even more awful from that angle.

They snuck down through the back service hall to look. What they saw made them even more in awe of Eddie than they'd been before—the dark room and Eddie all alone in it, pinned like a prisoner on his bed. He was a boy so terrible on the outside that he had to be kept in darkness. He was a boy so terrible on the inside he had to be tied down. He must be a horrible monster!

Riley thought about Eddie day and night and went with the other boys from Room 312 two or three times a day to stand in fear and wonder outside Eddie's solemn, nearly pitch-black room. He tried to imagine ever talking to Eddie but he couldn't. He did, though, want to see that face again—he wanted to feel how confused Eddie's face made him feel, just to test himself. Eddie's face was just like the match that started Riley's fire—Riley felt compelled to see more of it in the same way he'd felt compelled to strike that match. He wanted to see what the consequences would be. Would Eddie's face always terrify him? And if it did, would his own face—reported by Melvin Pitts to be just like Eddie's—do the same thing to other people?

22

Not much later, Riley got his wish. By then the excitement over Eddie had died down in the stir of other events that had come up. On Thursday, the doctor had announced that Parker's ankle was healed up enough so he could go home and he was leaving on Saturday. Miss MacGwyn was going around and oohing and ahhing to everybody all over the Acute Ward about how her Parker had been healed by God shortly after the priest had *a-nointed* him and how God was giving them a very special blessing by allowing them to go home. *It's a miracle!* she said every ten minutes and she said how just everybody she knew had put Parker on their prayers lists and how they'd been praying and praying and now God had answered all the prayers of all those dear *dear* people!

Riley was unable to get his mother's attention, the whole business had put her into such a stew—she even went home early that day—but it didn't really matter because he had other things on his mind: the doctors and the nurses seemed to be pressing in on him about his own face and everybody was studying his cheek to do a graft, which meant yet another surgery. And worse—much worse—the friendship-with-Melvin question had reared its ugly head again. What would he do without Parker MacGwyn there? He'd have to be friends with Melvin. He'd be stuck with him and he couldn't bear the thought of it.

On Friday afternoon he wandered down to the playroom by himself, his stomach a mess. It was right after lunch. His mother had dutifully taken Corliss and Kingsley MacGwyn out to a restaurant nearby in recognition of their departure and Carnell was asleep and Melvin and Parker were in some sort of angry standoff over the TV and wouldn't talk to each other or to Riley.

He didn't go the back way—he'd forgotten momentarily about Eddie and his face. He was hoping that the playroom would be empty and that he could take a pool cue and push the balls into the pockets without some other kid telling him he didn't know what he was doing.

But people were already in the playroom—he could hear their voices as he came along the hall. He thought about just sitting there in the hall on one of the wide window ledges, but that hallway always made him queasy because of the strong smell of sour strawberry milk so he decided he would go over in the corner of the playroom and pretend to read a book so whoever was in there would leave him alone and he'd have time to think things over about Melvin. He would have to make a decision soon about being his friend and *if* he decided he wouldn't be his friend—which seemed like it would be almost impossible—he would have to come up with some pretty good reasons.

But—*O God*—there weren't any! There weren't any good reasons to leave a person friendless!

He turned the corner into the playroom and there was Eddie. Riley's soul shuddered, just like it had the first time he'd seen Eddie's face, an inward rippling that started in his chest and reached right down to the ends of his fingertips in surprise and shock—and Eddie was looking right at him. But Riley didn't look too long because on either side of Eddie were two girls—two of the most beautiful girls Riley had ever seen in his life and they were laughing and fussing over Eddie as if he were the handsomest boy in the world. One of the girls had red hair that was cut short and she had very big lips and freckles all over her face. Her red hair made him think of Sarah back home, only Sarah's hair wasn't short. The other girl had long hair the color of sunflowers. Her eyes were wide open and they looked straight at Riley.

Hi! she said to him.

What's your name? said the other girl, the one with the big lips.

His name is Riley, said Eddie, before Riley could say a word—just as if he'd known Riley all his life. Eddie's voice was completely different than Riley had expected. He thought it would be mean and that it would come spitting out of Eddie's mouth full of bad words. But Eddie had a nice voice, deep like Riley's own father's.

How did you know my name? Riley asked him.

I asked the nurse who you were.

She knew me?

Eddie's voice was *very* nice, one of the nicest Riley thought he'd ever heard. Everybody knows you, Riley.

He could hardly comprehend the fact that everybody knew him, though he tried to give it a shape. He knew that Mr. Loflin and Gene and Miss Miranda and the other nurses knew him. He knew that Dr. Walker knew him—and the tub men, the OTs who made his splints, Miss Washington who made him move his arms all the time, the ladies who cleaned the hallways, the boys in his room—but he didn't think there was anybody outside of the Acute Ward who thought about him at all—except to act like they didn't want to talk to him—let alone knew him. And here one of the nurses on the Reconstruction Ward knew his name and she had told it to Eddie because

Eddie wanted to know who Riley was! Riley was stunned. This was news, important news, the kind of news you took back to your bed and thought about just before you went to sleep—news on a par with Jim Hawkins getting to go to Treasure Island or the revelation of Long John Silver's true nature or Lazarus coming forth alive from the dark cave.

The girl with the red hair and freckles wanted to know if Riley liked to play pool and if he wanted to play a game with the three of them. Nobody at the hospital had ever asked Riley to play pool. He always had to ask if he could play and then kids almost always said no.

They spent the next hour playing pool and talking and laughing and the two girls teased Eddie and talked to him as if he were the most wonderful, kindest, best boy in the whole world and not a boy whose face sent shivers down their spines. They were Eddie's sisters, it turned out, and the way they acted it seemed like there was nobody in the world who measured up to Eddie and they would dare anybody to say otherwise.

Being with Eddie all that time gave Riley a chance to study his face carefully. It was—really and truly—a terrible face. It didn't look like the face of a person. It looked like the face of a monster. It was horrifying and fascinating by turns. Riley would look at Eddie's face and study it until it became familiar. Then he'd look down at the pool table to hit his ball, then up again and he would be horrified once more. He'd have to get used to it all over again. The skin on Eddie's face was very tight and shiny in some places. In some spots it was puffy and bumpy, like around his mouth. He didn't seem to have any lips at all—his face went from skin to teeth—and his eyes were ringed around on either side and above and below with patches of skin. Each patch was a different color. Eddie had little pieces of hair sticking out of his head but mostly he was bald and his nose was bent over to the right and seemed to have only one hole, not two, but Riley couldn't be sure because he didn't dare stare at Eddie too much.

Eddie wanted to know more about Riley: did Riley like the hospital and did Riley like the food and did Riley like the nurses and did Riley know Mr. Loflin and what did he think of him and how about Dr. Walker and which of the residents and interns did Riley like the best and how did Riley feel about surgery? Skin grafts? Tubs? What about Jackson and Johnson? Did Riley like them? Had he heard about Pat and her Uncle Jimmy?—Eddie had met Pat the first day he was here. Had Riley met them yet?

Eddie said he'd been coming to the hospital for almost

ten years and he knew everybody here and he liked all of them, Mr. Loflin included, and that the hospital was like home to him, and that his sisters always tried to come to the hospital with him, though they couldn't always come the whole time. This time they had only been able to come after the surgery because they were both in school and this time they told their parents to stay home until it was time to come get Eddie, they were old enough to take care of Eddie by themselves and their parents could take a break.

How old are you? Riley wanted to know.

I'm sixteen.

Eddie's face was so hard to look at that after a while all you really saw were his eyes and his mouth. His eyes were warm and brown and soft and he always looked straight at you. They were always smiling.

Riley liked him. He liked him very much and before he left that day, he asked Eddie if they could play pool again the next day. And Eddie said that was a good idea, and that if everything in his new graft was healing the way it was supposed to, he would meet him in the playroom at the same time tomorrow.

When he got back to the room, Melvin wanted to know where he'd been and how come he stayed away so long, and Riley told Melvin and Parker that he'd been playing pool with Eddie, the boy who'd been electrocuted, and that Eddie was really very nice. Melvin pressed his hands up against his face and groaned, as if Riley now had a disease caught directly from Eddie the monster—the disease of monsterness. Parker and Carnell wanted to know what Eddie said and Parker especially wanted to know about his two sisters. Riley said he would introduce all of them to Eddie, if they wanted, so the four of them left immediately for the playroom, but Eddie wasn't there. He wasn't in his room, either, or down on the second floor or in the cafeteria or anywhere. And because they couldn't meet Eddie for themselves, the roommates felt some cause to doubt Riley's story.

He's not a nice boy, Melvin said when they got back to their room. He's mean, I know it. He's a terrible boy. You want everybody to like him because you look like him, Riley. You're a liar, Liar!

How you know that, Melvin? Carnell giggled. You too afraid to talk to Eddie.

No, I'm not! Melvin declared. I'm not afraid of anything, especially a boy who hasn't got anything that looks like a nose on his face. How can you stand him, Riley? said Melvin. He's horrible!

He's my friend, said Riley firmly, and didn't feel the need to pay any more attention to Melvin after that.

23

That night Riley could hardly sleep for thinking of all the marvelous events that had occurred that day. He had met Eddie face to face! And instead of being awful, Eddie was really nice! He played back every sighting of his face, from the first terrifying pull at his insides when he walked into the playroom through each subsequent look. Every time he was surprised. It was such a terrible face—the scars were just—a mess—really, it was the most disorderly piecing together of skin—but in the looking, in the continuous looking, it never lost its terror—it never lost its terror—it just became, oh, Riley didn't know, he didn't have the words, he just loved Eddie—Eddie had been so kind—he had been the first person at the hospital who had been really kind to him—and thought he was probably the handsomest boy he'd ever known—the thought had suddenly slipped into his mind: the handsomest boy. Yes.

He wished he could call and tell his father about Eddie.

Even though Eddie was sixteen and Riley was only seven, Eddie had talked to Riley like they were friends and Riley thought maybe Eddie could be the best friend at the hospital that he'd been searching for—better than Parker—and anyway, Parker was leaving in the morning.

And Eddie had been just about his own age when he'd gotten electrocuted. Had he stood out in the lightning on purpose? Did he understand about destiny? Did he see how it was that Superman lost himself forever by kissing Lois Lane? Riley would ask Eddie the next time he saw him.

Riley was so excited about Eddie, he could hardly think. He turned on his reading light and pretended to read his favorite section of *Treasure Island*—he knew it by heart from listening to the tape—the part where Jim Hawkins ran off and single-handedly saved the day—though when Jim first set out it didn't look anything but foolish (the doctor was mad at him). But Jim knew!

It reminded Riley of how it was with his fire—how to his parents it all seemed like a big mistake and that Riley didn't know anything, but one day they would see.

Superman was one thing, but Jim Hawkins—a boy

just like himself—*probably big for his age*—courageous, imaginative, snappy, at the ready, inventive, clever, strong, adventurous—though maybe older—was another whole thing altogether. Jim Hawkins didn't need a cape and a mask. He didn't have to hide his identity. He just got by on his wits. Riley wondered if Eddie knew about Jim Hawkins and about Treasure Island and all the things that went on there and he fell asleep that night thinking that in the morning he would go talk to Eddie and see how Eddie felt about fire and destiny and he dreamed about Eddie all night long.

In his dreams, he and Eddie poked silently along the hospital halls while everyone else was fast asleep—

—NOT A SOUL STIRS.

Riley and Eddie take their time going in and out of every room. It is just like being on Treasure Island—dark, desolate, utterly quiet—though with some high spots—*yap! yap! yap!* Lady Luck comes bounding down the hallway, her little toes clicking on the shiny floor. She sits patiently, her tail wagging, while Eddie and Riley play a game of pool in the playroom and paint a long, tall mural on the playroom wall that they call *The Destruction of the Known Universe*, complete with dinosaurs, Superman, Wonder Woman, the Bionic Man,

Lazarus coming out of his tomb with funeral rags flying off, two triumphant boys—masked and armored—and a trusty dog eating out of a golden bowl.

Then Greg appears. Lady Luck jumps up and spins around in a dainty pirouette. Eddie is delighted. He knows instantly that Greg is Riley's best friend and even more instantly, they all three become best friends together and immediately they decide to leave the playroom so that Eddie and Riley can show Greg the sorts of things that only boys who are burned—inside and out—know.

Like—the hallway leading down to the surgery room.

Eddie flips on the lights. Everything is revealed and!—at their disposal. Operating table, surgical instruments, control panels, stainless-steel shelves and cabinets. Let's put on gowns, Eddie suggests. They soap up to their elbows, put on rubber gloves.

Who shall we work on first? Riley wants to know.

What about you, Riley? says Eddie.

Me? says Riley. Is there a problem? Greg and Eddie study Riley for a long time. Information passes between them like light.

What do you see, Greg? Eddie wants to know.

Well, it's not what I remember Riley looking like, says Greg, but . . . he looks fine to me.

Well, says Eddie, what about Carnell Hughes then?

They saunter down the hall to get Carnell.

Okay then, let's begin. First they put Carnell's fingers on. Easy. Just copy the ones on his good hand, make duplicates, stick them on, just like brand new. Whoops! They're backward. Turn them around. Then his ear. They fix his hair—tug the good hair a little to cover up that bald part. They rub their hands all over Carnell's chest, up and along his arm. *Whoooo*, Eddie blows out of his lips as his hands go round and round. All done.

Got Carnell fixed up, says Greg with satisfaction. He's good to go.

Well, not quite, says Riley. He needs a mother.

He doesn't have a mother?

Well, he does, says Riley, but she's in jail, and his grandmother's too old, so they don't exactly know what to do with him, which is why he's been here so long. But no sooner were the words out of his mouth, then down at the end of the hall came the nicest looking lady with the biggest smile and her arms wide open, calling out *Carnell! Carnell, baby!* And Carnell was gone.

Let's do someone else. They walk along from bed to bed.

Here's Pat, all chalky-white and wrapped around in shivering sheets, looking almost like a dead person except that she shakes so.

I know this one, Eddie, says Riley. It's Pat, the mean girl.

She's dead? asks Greg.

She was dead, says Eddie.

She was? says Riley. He didn't remember her being dead. The last time he'd seen her, she was very much alive. Well, sort of.

Not now, says Eddie. He touches her with his hand, a lovely smile appears on her richly colored face, little bubbles of spit pop out of her mouth, and she says hi and gets up and dances away.

Then there's Melvin. The three of them stand over his bed. Before they do a thing, Riley tells Greg and Eddie everything about the painful friendship business: how he sees that Melvin has no friends—but he—Riley—feels like he should be Melvin's friend because he thinks being friendless is horrible and because he remembers the terrible time when Jason and Sarah ran down the street with Greg and they were having so much fun and he was alone by himself in the house—*do you remember that, Greg?*—but he is so afraid to be Melvin's friend because Melvin is so . . . Melvin, and right as he's talking, Eddie says, I'll be his friend, too, Riley, and then Greg has the most brilliant idea: Let's just fix him up, Riley. Then he can go home and you won't have to think about him ever again.

Well, here's the trouble, Greg. I don't know if his mother and father are ready to take him back, even if we fix him up.

But—Lady Luck is barking. Riley and Greg and Eddie look out the window. Down below, at the hospital's front door, waiting for visiting hours, are Harry Pitts and his wife, come to take Melvin away. Quick, says Eddie. They go to fixing and fixing and in a heartbeat, Melvin is cured. They pack his suitcase, throw in a couple of games from the playroom, carry him downstairs in his sleep—*No point in waking him up, is there?*—and stuff him in the backseat of his father's car.

24

On Saturday, Parker's mother arrived very early, dressed in a fancy yellow sweater, some pearls around her neck. Kingsley MacGwyn was downstairs with their Cadillac, ready to load up Parker's things, which Parker's mother started packing in boxes, moving slowly and most carefully so, she said, she wouldn't break any of her fingernails. She had removed her gold bracelets, all of them, so they wouldn't get hurt.

The car! yelled Melvin Pitts all of a sudden. The remote-controlled car! You're not taking the remote-controlled car? he screamed.

Shut up, Melvin, said Parker. That car is mine.

Would you pipe down, Melvin? said Parker's mother. Please. I am trying to pack up so we can take Parker home.

Who am I going to play with if Parker goes home? Melvin interrupted. Did you think of that? My mother and father aren't here and I don't have any friends and now you're leaving and who will I play with?

Riley and Carnell are here, said Miss MacGwyn. Play with Riley and Carnell.

I don't want to play with Riley and Carnell. I don't like Riley, he looks like a monster, and Carnell's a nigger. I only like Parker.

Riley dear, said Parker's mother so sweetly, can I leave Parker's last bag of M&Ms with you?

I want some M&Ms! Melvin croaked. Hey, what about me?

Nothing for you, Melvin, said Parker's mother, putting the candy down on Riley's bed. If you won't be nice, you won't get a thing.

I am nice! Yes, I am, I am nice.

No, you're not! You don't know a thing about nice.

You're the pits, Melvin, said Parker. Face it.

I don't have time to bother with this, said Parker's mother. I've got to get Parker's things ready for Kingsley and we've got to talk to Dr. Walker one more time.

Parker's things were packed long before the doctor ever showed up. Kingsley made a bunch of trips up and down the elevator with Parker's boxes. The MacGwyns stood around and waited, Miss MacGwyn peering at her watch over the edge of her glasses every few minutes, her bracelets back on and jingling. Riley's mother showed up around ten, just about the time Mr. Loflin came in yelling that Uncle Jimmy had left.

Up and gone, he said. *Said Pat's too mean for him to deal with.*

Pat, having met Riley's mother that one day in the playroom, decided that she wanted to move into Room 312 to be near her, especially since she'd heard there was now a bed opening up. She made Uncle Jimmy tell the nurse to move her, but Jimmy said the nurse said not until Pat learned to eat by herself and not until she walked by herself and went to the bathroom by herself and not until she stopped scratching her grafts so they would heal.

I ain't got no fingers to eat with, whined Mr. Loflin in a perfect imitation of Pat. *They took all my fingers. Ask them where my fingers is. And my feets hurt so bad, I can't walk and I can't get to the bathroom.*

Uncle Jimmy also told Pat that the nurse told him that she could eat even if she had no fingers, said they could fix something up so she could do it.

Uncle Jimmy also told Pat that the nurse told him that they could teach Pat how to walk again and until then, when Pat had to pee, she should call them and they would help her to the toilet. Uncle Jimmy told Pat she better hurry up and figure all these things out because he wasn't going to be staying with her much longer. Said he had business to take care of back in Dallas.

The whole thing had made Pat so mad, Mr. Loflin reported, that she decided *she* wanted to kill somebody.

So, said Mr. Loflin, she cussed at Uncle Jimmy, telling him that he was supposed to kill all these people and get her out of here and take her back home so she could live with him and why wasn't he doing anything?

She went completely backward. She quit eating. She spit everything out. She didn't tell anyone she had to pee, she just peed in her bed.

On Friday afternoon, Jimmy got up and said, You gonna have to take care of yourself from now on, girl.

Where you going? Pat had cried.

I'm gone, Jimmy said.

And he walked out the door and didn't look back!

Mr. Loflin stuck his neck out at Parker MacGwyn. *What do you think of them apples, Parker? That mean gal's her own worst enemy.*

After this recital and Miss MacGwyn's commentary on the same, Saturday morning cartoons kept the four boys' attention for a while, but when the shows were over, they fidgeted and complained. There was nowhere to go. The playroom was closed all day because the playroom lady was sick. And there was nothing to do but wait for the doctor to tell Parker he could go home. Parker's parents and Riley's mother made small talk with lots of empty spaces in between. Riley could tell that his mother was ready for Miss MacGwyn to leave.

Riley Martin was miserable. The euphoria from the day before had disappeared. Since the playroom wasn't open, he wasn't sure how he would see Eddie again. He didn't feel like he could go to Eddie's room. And Parker was leaving and he'd never proved to him—or to Melvin or Carnell—that he'd actually seen Eddie or talked to him or played pool with him, and Parker had never even had the chance to see Eddie's two beautiful sisters. And Riley had only dreamed that Eddie was his best friend—he didn't have any promises in reality.

Carnell Hughes kept pestering Riley with questions and finally Riley had to tell him to be quiet. He had to think. Parker was leaving and that meant he and Carnell were stuck with Melvin Pitts. He had talked to his mother about her possibly talking to the head nurse, seeing if maybe . . .

No, his mother said right away. Don't even think about it. We'll be leaving in another few weeks and I'm not moving again. You'll be fine. And your father will be here in just a while, right after he gets off the shuttle from the airport.

Hopefully he won't get here before the MacGwyns leave, she muttered.

Another few weeks! It seemed like an eternity. Every minute with Melvin Pitts was torture. He didn't know how he would be able to stand it. And Melvin even said he didn't like him. And called him a monster. And now his father was coming, a normally joyous event, except that his father would want him to be as "nice as possible" to Melvin, at least until he left on Sunday, and during that nice-as-possible time, Melvin might get the idea that Riley was going to be his best friend on a permanent basis.

What a mess!

Then finally Dr. Walker arrived in his Saturday slacks and shirt and said Parker was good to go and the nurses on duty came in the room to say good-bye and everybody shook Parker's hand and said what a nice boy he was and thanked his mother and father for everything they had done for the hospital and Mr. Loflin came in and made a loud, scratchy speech about what fine folks the MacGwyns were and what an addition Parker had made to Room 312. Parker's mother went and hugged

Riley's mother and told her to write *any* time and come visit *whenever* she and her husband and Riley were in Louisiana and that she was *so* thankful that God had healed her Parker and then Parker's mother blew Riley a kiss and said how much she *loved* him and what a wonderful, brave boy he was—all things considered—and gave Riley the remote control and wiggled her fingers at Carnell as she stood by the door. Parker waved at Riley and Carnell from across the room. He didn't even look at Melvin. And Kingsley gave Riley's mother a little kiss on the cheek, just barely missing her nose and turned red and shook Riley's hand and said *Be strong, young man*, and gave Carnell a little tap on his good arm and said *Bye, Tiger*, and went over to Melvin and said firmly *Okay now, Melvin, it's up to you*, and Melvin screamed bloody murder and Kingsley shut the door behind him and the remaining roommates watched—from one set of windows to another—as the MacGwyns wheeled Parker out of the Acute Ward for good.

25

Thirty minutes after Parker MacGwyn left with his mother and father, Melvin Pitts quieted down all of a sudden and asked if Riley and Carnell wanted to play a game and if so, what game? And wondered did Carnell know tomorrow's Bible verse and asked Carnell which of the cartoons that morning he had liked the best and wondered if Riley would introduce him to Eddie, and didn't say a word about Eddie being a monster. Carnell asked Melvin was he sick or something, and Melvin said he just now felt better than he'd ever felt in his life. Riley waited a while to see if Melvin's new ways would last—he didn't feel like being tricked—and then, having waited long enough—at least ten minutes—with Riley's mother asleep in the chair beside Riley's bed, the three of them—Riley, Melvin, and Carnell—sat down on the floor and brought out the Monopoly board—it was Riley's choice—and played by many different rules, some of them Melvin's, some of them Riley's, some of them Carnell's—and all of them, for that hour at least, acceptable.

And just shortly after that game ended, Riley's father showed up and everyone was—mostly—glad to see him.

His father had come bearing gifts—crayons and a coloring book for Carnell, a *Wonder Woman* comic book for Melvin, lemon drops and candy bars for all three boys, a blank yellow notebook for Riley's mother with her name on the cover made by some friend of a friend who had heard about the fire. And a round pillow for Riley with a sad face stitched in blue thread on one side and a happy face stitched in red on the other, made by the wife of a man Lewis worked with at Fort Bliss. He also had school photos and little bits and pieces of news from Bertha and Arturo next door and from the Favelas next door to them. And a flowery card from the Coulehans across the street that said something about God and Truth, with a capital G in cursive. His mother took one look at it and shoved it in the drawer of Riley's nightstand.

What's the matter? his father wanted to know.

I've heard enough about God to last a lifetime! his mother spit out. And then she started to cry, even though Melvin and Carnell were sitting right there staring at her.

Corliss MacGwyn had this priest come to pray over Parker. And then on Thursday—his mother sobbed—*after the doctor came in and said Parker could go home, Corliss MacGwyn went around telling everybody that Parker had been healed by God!*

Cynthia, his father said. Come on. Not now.

Why not right now? she yelled at him. *I could have killed her!* Why the hell doesn't God heal Riley? His mother and father both turned toward him. His father's eyes were looking wild, like they sometimes did when his mother got going like this. Carnell leaned up against the bed, picking at something on the sheet. Melvin stood there with his mouth open, breathing loud.

It's Riley who needs healing, his mother said. Not Parker. *It's Riley!*—don't you understand? Parker is spoiled. The only thing that got burned on his body is his ankle. He didn't get healed. It just healed up on its own, the way things do. But Corliss went around telling *every*one that GAWD—you know how she says it!— had visited Parker—she wouldn't know GAWD if he flew right in her face—and everyone was listening to her and smiling and smiling and saying *Why, praise God!*—his mother opened her mouth in a ghoulish smile—because Corliss wears expensive clothes and pearls around her neck and bright-red lipstick and matching nail polish.

She even went down and told the damn dietitian, that stupid lady who is so easily impressed by anybody. *God almighty!* She just told everybody—she even told the people in the kitchen!

His mother cried and cried. Carnell Hughes brought over a box of Kleenex and she sat crying and blowing her nose.

Oh, maybe God did heal Parker, she whispered after a while—between sobs. Maybe he did heal Parker and one miracle at this godforsaken place is all he's about to perform.

And then she cried some more.

Honey, his father said. Why don't you take the afternoon off—take a nap, or go for a walk along the Seawall?

I don't want to take a walk! she snapped. I hate this place, she said, and then got up and left the room.

HIS MOTHER SEEMED LIKE she wasn't really there all weekend. She came to visit Riley with his father, just like always, but she just stared at the two of them talking as if she was a million miles away.

What are you thinking about? his father asked her.

Oh, nothing, she said. She blinked and went right back to staring straight ahead.

On Sunday, his father sat in a chair with his arms propped up on Riley's bed and ran on with news of home—*Laura Miller was planning to have an Art Show to celebrate Riley's return—they would put the paintings up all over Riley's front porch—Greg was already working on his drawing—Sarah and her sister Mary were coloring princesses with sparkling golden crowns*—as if not a single thing in the whole world had changed, especially his mother.

At one point, she sighed really loud and glared at them, so his father suggested that he and all the boys go down to the playroom for a game of pool.

Riley's father left on Sunday afternoon. The plan was that he would return just one more time, since Riley was to have his last surgery on the coming Thursday. If all went well, Riley and his mother would be able to come home within a week after that. Whenever that happened, Lewis would fly down to Galveston and help them make the trip back to El Paso.

The minute his father left, Riley's mother seemed to perk up. Her best friend Betsy was coming from Albuquerque to spend the next week with her. She was, in fact, so excited about Betsy's arrival the following afternoon that she decided to leave the hospital early and go back to her apartment to strip the beds and change the sheets and clean so everything would be just right.

It will really be great to see her, his mother told him. I can't wait. I have so much to tell her.

She looked over at Melvin and Carnell. You kids will love my friend Betsy, she said.

26

And it was true. They all loved Betsy. Everything about Betsy was to love. She was tall, as tall as Riley's father almost, and she was big all around like a man and she had long legs and walked with great, long strides. She wore her hair pulled back in a bun, but it never stayed in place. It was always flying all around her head and she wore clothes with bright colors and when she moved, it was sure and steady and certain. Not nervous and high-strung, like Miss MacGwyn.

Betsy was a librarian. She loved to read out loud or to make up stories as she went along. She liked to sing and she was a listener, too. And, according to his mother, that's why she had come: Betsy was there to listen, because, his mother had said, she had so much to tell her.

Riley wondered what exactly, because it seemed to him that whatever his mother had to say she'd already said to Miss MacGwyn or to his father or to the nurses—

or to that priest—when they came in. Or to Marilyn Hooper, the psychiatrist who was burned herself, who came up sometimes to talk to him—or who invited his mother down to visit her. Or to the lady in the playroom.

His mother seemed to talk to just about everybody she met, telling everybody every single thing about herself and about Riley. As a matter of fact, Riley wished she didn't talk so much. Sometimes she talked loud enough so Riley could hear her or so loud that everybody else could, too, or sometimes she whispered or went and stood outside the room to talk, resting her chin on her hand, her shoulders bent over, staring down at the floor. That's how she talked to the doctors and nurses, as if they were hitting her over the head with their news. Riley could see her through the glass windows. He couldn't figure out why she was so upset all the time. He wished she'd laugh—just once in a while. Maybe now that Betsy was here, she would.

BETSY WAS VERY GLAD to see him. She was so glad, her eyes filled up with tears the minute she came into the room. So did his. Betsy looked just perfect, her smile so big and her hair all frizzing out around her head, a big red scarf around her neck.

Riley, dear, I've missed you so, she said right away.

Can I hug you? Where can I touch you? Just the sound of her voice made him happy.

She had brought him a sweater. She had just finished knitting it, she told him. It was bright blue and she'd made it extra big for next winter because she knew he'd be taller by then. All the time she was knitting, she was thinking of him. It was a beautiful sweater.

Betsy and his mother stayed in Room 312 all that first afternoon. His mother kept telling Betsy to rest, to take a break, but Betsy wouldn't do it. She said she wanted to spend the time with Riley and she didn't need a break of any sort. She said she'd brought all sorts of books and stories to read and she wanted Riley to tell her all about his time at the hospital. She was glad to meet Melvin and Carnell, too, and she set right in to include them in her conversations and to find all there was to know about them.

Right in the middle of Betsy's first afternoon, they even had a visit from Pat, who entered in a wheelchair pushed by Mr. Loflin.

Here she comes, the old mean girl. Says she wants to see you, Miss Martin.

And in comes Pat. She was breathing hard, just as if she'd been running, and she made Mr. Loflin push her right up in front of Riley's mother.

Who's this? she demanded, looking at Betsy. This a boy or a girl?

I'm a girl, Betsy laughed.

You fat, Pat said.

Nice girl, Mr. Loflin sang out. Come on now, girl. You ain't got nothing good to say, you come back with me.

But Pat wanted to tell Riley's mother about Jimmy leaving and about how she, Pat, was going to leave, too, she was going to up and walk out of this place, only she said it so fast that nobody could understand.

Oh, she's just mad about Jimmy, is all, said Mr. Loflin. She wants to leave, says she's going to get up one day and get out of here.

Is Jimmy your father? asked Betsy.

I ain't got a father, Pat cried. Jimmy's my uncle and he's gone!

You're wearing out your welcome, girl. Come on, now.

But Pat stayed in Room 312 most of the afternoon, not saying much, but listening hard and chiming in every little bit with the sort of things mean girls say, like that she didn't have nobody to help her and that people were telling her what to do all day long.

Betsy had a little black plastic comb in her purse and when Pat saw that, she started fussing and crying.

What do you want? Betsy asked her.

I wants that comb, Pat wailed, and I wants to move into that bed, she said, pointing at the very spot where Parker used to sleep.

Betsy gave her the comb, tucking it into the pocket of Pat's gown.

About the bed, though, Pat, said Riley's mother. The nurses said you can't move in here until you eat and walk all by yourself. You better pay attention to them or you'll never get over here. And you better hurry because Riley and I aren't going to be here for long. We're going home, she said, her lips pinched together. We're going home real soon.

Sometimes in the afternoons that week, Betsy would come to Room 312 by herself, spending the time reading books to Riley and Melvin and Carnell, or telling them stories that they'd never heard before. The churning in Riley's stomach stopped altogether—he felt certain he could even drink strawberry milk again—and even when the tub men told him that Eddie Rabedeaux had already left to go home, it didn't matter, because he knew that he was leaving soon himself.

Wednesday morning, his mother went down to talk to the discharge nurse who would tell her how to take care of Riley when he was at home. It was a long time before she got back. By then, Melvin had gone to play pool and Carnell was in the tubs, and so Riley had Betsy all to himself. He told her all about *Treasure Island* and the part that gave him the creeps—the revelation of Long John Silver's true nature—he turned out to be such a terrible character—disguised in the body of a really nice pirate!

His mother came in the room all excited. Riley looked up—what was different about her? New clothes? No. Lipstick? No. She had a big smile on her face. Riley figured maybe it was all that talking she and Betsy were doing at night and having her friend here and being glad that soon she and Riley would go home. Seeing her so happy made Riley feel perfectly happy. He climbed up on his bed just to sit and watch his mother and her best friend talking and before he knew it he was half asleep, the sound of their voices shifting in and out of his head.

She had this priest come here.

And thus began—again!—the story of the man who came to visit Parker, the one Parker's mother had invited.

He was an Episcopal priest—*of course,* his mother went on—*Corliss being Corliss*—tall, straight as a post, handsome—*almost too handsome—they must all be like that.* The priest at the Episcopal church down the street from the Martins, the place they sometimes went, was the same way—elegant and perfumed and very with-it—*rides a motorcycle and goes folk dancing with his wife.* And there was Corliss, oohing and ahhing. Poor Parker—*Parker Parker Parker Parker*—and Corliss laughed a funny ha-ha sort of laugh and gave the priest a very big smile. *Could the Father please a-noint him*—his mother whispered—*almost as if she were inviting him to sleep with her instead of heal her son.*

She drove me crazy!

And then his mother told Betsy how the priest had put the oil on Parker's head and how he had started to leave and then how he had looked over—*finally*—in her direction.

He knew I'd been staring at him. I wonder if he could tell how much I despised Corliss right then. I wonder if he could smell my anger. The minute he looked at me, I started to cry. I went and told him everything—that it was Riley who needed healing—not Parker—and he put his hands on Riley's bandages—not on Riley's hands—he wouldn't touch Riley—he kept his hands waving around Riley's head—and prayed and then left and didn't even look back.

He didn't even look back! his mother said again. She thought he should have looked back. Actually, with what she had told him, she thought he should have sat down there in the room and waited to see how his prayer turned out. It didn't matter how long it took. *He was a priest, wasn't he? Isn't that what a priest's job is, to wait and see how his prayers get answered?*

But he left. *Good riddance!*

Riley's mother said that Corliss' priest was just exactly like the priest in El Paso—*that's why I hate church.* The priest in El Paso didn't talk to kids, for one thing. He didn't like them, that was obvious. And he wasn't going to waste even a minute on Riley now—*oh no!*—he ministered to handsome supplicants only—and sinners with money!

Doesn't matter, she concluded. *I'm not taking Riley to that stupid church anyway. That fey and fancy priest in El Paso won't ever even get the chance to ignore him.*

27

Riley drifted off and woke up again to hear the hum of his mother's voice telling Betsy about a dream she'd had early one morning. He was in it. He kept his eyes shut so she would think he was still asleep.

In her dream, his face was covered with patches of skin, all different colors. His eye was pulled down and his nose was gone and he was looking at her and smiling real big, as if, she said, this was the face he'd wanted all along, as if this face with all the patches was his real face and his other face had just been a mask. Apparently Riley wasn't the only person in the dream: there were all sorts of people standing around smiling real big too, and all those people were watching his mother, waiting for her to understand what they already knew.

Then she and Riley were standing in front of God and she was holding Riley up by the shoulder of his t-shirt and was telling God to heal him, to put his face back the way it was. She told God that she would go to church, and that she would stop drinking beer, and that she would be kind to people, but as soon as the words came out of her mouth, she knew that she wouldn't be able to keep her promises.

Riley's stomach knotted up. This worry of his mother's about her promises reminded him a lot of all the stewing he had done about Melvin. *Should he be his friend or shouldn't he be his friend*?—back and forth, back and forth. All that worrying just served to make him know how hopeless the situation was. He just didn't want to be Melvin's friend! *Ever ever ever!*

His mother said that—in her dream—she told God that she was sorry she was so angry at Riley.

But as soon as she told God she was sorry, she knew it wasn't true—she was *so* angry at Riley. And she wasn't sorry.

Riley leaned in to listen a little closer.

In her dream, she begged God to give Riley back his old face. She said she got down on her knees, every bit of her, and begged God to fix Riley. She begged him. She grabbed his feet. She wasn't going to let him go until he put Riley back together.

The dream had been a terrible dream, his mother told Betsy. She couldn't figure out if she was awake or asleep, if it was really happening or if she was dreaming. She could hear the dew dripping and shifting through the smooth green leaves of Mrs. Griswald's magnolia trees outside the window of her apartment and then, after a while, she felt someone holding her close. *Had his father come?* But there was no one with her. She fell back asleep while this person who wasn't there rocked her back and forth, just like a baby.

Boy! His father had said his mother was taking all this pretty hard, but it seemed that she was also imagining things!

And then suddenly, she said, she couldn't breathe. She sat straight up in her bed, pressing her hand against her chest, her heart ached so.

I could feel their presence all around me. We were together again around the dining room table back home, sitting and daydreaming like we had been the morning of the fire, empty coffee cups and milk glasses, plates almost clean of Aunt Jemima's syrup and little bits of pancakes, Riley playing a game of Monopoly with Lewis, me watching and thinking how perfect we all were. Everything was perfect—Riley's face, his beautiful face, his incredible auburn hair. We were back like we were before the fire happened.

Riley's mother leaned in and peered at her friend

Betsy. *Except that it had happened, and it was after the fire, and now everything had been restored just like it was before. Riley had been healed. Do you understand?*

Nobody said anything for a while after that.

Then his mother said: *Don't you think that dream was a sign that God would heal Riley?*

Betsy studied his mother's face really hard. So did he—while still pretending to be asleep. Her face was bright red and her eyes were watery.

Betsy touched his mother's hand and said, Don't you think you shouldn't get your hopes up too much, dear?

What do you mean? his mother said. What do you think I'm hoping? Her voice was shaking.

Well, I know you're hoping for a miracle, but . . . maybe you shouldn't . . .

Why? Do you think God can't heal Riley? Corliss said he healed Parker and Parker wasn't hardly even burned. Do you think God can't heal Riley because he set himself on fire? Do you think that people who set themselves on fire don't need healing just as much as anyone else? Is that it? Parker set himself on fire, too. Parker was drinking.

Betsy sat for a long time and then shook her head. I just don't have any answers, Cindy, she said. None at all, but I can't help thinking that we don't really know what healing looks like.

I know exactly what it looks like! his mother snapped back. It looks like Riley with his nose back, Riley with hair on his head, us back home around the dining room table. That's what it looks like, Betsy. That's the picture God gave me—*and that's what it's going to look like!*

And she started crying. Again.

28

Betsy's visit—though wonderful—was not all sunshine and roses. Wednesday evening was clouded by the fact that in the morning he would have surgery. He hated surgery. You couldn't eat or drink anything after midnight and that rule alone made him long for Cokes and 7-Ups and ice-cream sundaes all through the night. He hated the hallway going down to surgery and the horrible smell of the surgery room itself with its near-blinding lights and the doctors all talking so loud like they were talking to a boy who didn't know anything when he felt certain—though he couldn't prove it—that he'd been in that surgery room more times than all of them combined. He hated the horrible-smelling mask they put over his face and the weird, awful sensation of being sucked into a far distant place he didn't want to go to. And then there was nothing. Not rest, not sleep, but no place. And then a terrible wrenching call back as if he were Lazarus himself: *Wake up, Riley! Wake up, Riley! Riley, would you wake up! Now, don't go back to sleep.*

And the desire to throw up. Which he always gave in to.

And then for the next week, a horrible burning pain in the place where they had taken the skin to graft onto an open space. And having to always sleep or sit so that the grafted skin wouldn't be disturbed.

The only thing that made it bearable was the thought that this was his last surgery—they were going to close up a large open spot on his back using skin they would take from his left thigh—and that he was going home soon. That and the fact that his mother was there very early in the morning, waiting in the room with him, Melvin and Carnell still asleep, the halls dark and quiet, the night nurses still on duty.

HE DIDN'T REMEMBER THURSDAY at all because even though the nurse got him to wake up, and even though he threw up, he still couldn't think straight. Friday morning wasn't much better by way of paying attention, but by Friday afternoon he was able to enjoy an invalid's vacation—Betsy and his mother—very distracted—just in from the afternoon spent at the Strand—

fussing over him a little more than usual, the nurses giving him just a little more attention.

Betsy told the boys all about the little stores they'd been in—junk stores and antique shops, a whole store full of books and comics, a store with a piano that played tinny songs all by itself. That place had a high counter where they served sundaes and sodas and Betsy and his mother had ordered Brown Cows with root beer and vanilla ice cream. Riley had never heard of Brown Cows. Neither had Melvin or Carnell.

That store had old-fashioned candy, too. Betsy brought back samples of different ones: Neccos and little dots of candy on long skinny sheets of paper and Jujubes. And Milky Ways. And comic books. And a copy of a Hardy Boys mystery called *Hunting for Hidden Gold,* which Betsy said she thought she could finish reading just before the Easter egg hunt on Sunday, because it was already Easter. *If they got started right then—*

Betsy read until *Wonder Woman* came on—*Frank and Joe Hardy's father had called them out west to search for a gang that was involved in a robbery*—and then stopped and then picked up again right after the show was over, until it was close to time for them to leave. His mother had been staring at Riley's face during much of Betsy's reading, but the minute Betsy got up to go to the bathroom before they left for home, she fumbled around in her purse and then told Riley to sit up on his bed. She stood very close to him, her back to the nurse's station, a little brown bottle in her hand—something like the brown bottle the priest had had—which she tipped back and forth. Her hand was shaking.

Hold still, she said, and then she began to rub the oil all around his eyes.

Riley pulled back. What are you doing, Mom? What's this?

Stop! she hissed. Sit still. This is vitamin E. I bought it at a health food store this afternoon. The lady said it would heal burns. She put some more on his cheeks and around his mouth.

Did you ask the doctor?

What does he know?

Does Betsy know you bought it?

I don't need to ask Betsy about this. Now, be quiet. It won't hurt you. It will make you feel better and in the morning, we'll do some more and your skin will get better and better. Then everyone will see.

See what?

You'll see. Now be quiet.

Betsy and his mother left right after that. And then the nursing staff changed and right after that Mr. Loflin came in screeching about it being time for them to go to bed.

What's going on with your face, Riley? he yelled for all to hear. What's all that shiny stuff? What're you doing, putting cream on it? You think you're the doctor now?

Riley tried to get Mr. Loflin to come over by his bed so he could whisper about the vitamin E, but that didn't work at all.

Your mother did this? Mr. Loflin said as loud as he could. What's she thinking? She can't do this! Vitamin E ain't going to do nothing. Okay, vitamin E, you got a sunburn or you got a teensy little burn on your finger. Maybe yes, vitamin E. But vitamin E for what you got—*no no no no!*

Mr. Loflin got a wet cloth and began to wash Riley's face very carefully. No no no no, can't be doing this. These grafts have got to rest until they heal. That old oil will just loosen them grafts. What's going on with your mother, boy? She's getting worn out, ain't she? *Poor gal. Bless her heart.*

THE NEXT MORNING, IT seemed like every doctor and nurse in the place had got the word about the vitamin E, because the minute Riley's mother and Betsy came in the room, they asked his mother to step into the nurse's station and Dr. Walker and the nurses began to talk and she stood there with her elbow on her arm and her chin on her hand and tears streaming down her face, looking like they were beating her to death.

Betsy continued on with *Hunting for Hidden Gold*, trying to get the boys' minds on something beside what was going on in the nurse's station.

His mother came in and sat down. She didn't say a word.

After a while Betsy stopped reading and asked his mother if she was okay.

Do they think I'm stupid? Riley is MY son, not theirs!

That was all she said for most of the morning, but just before lunch she got up and disappeared and about an hour later she came back. She said she'd been walking on the beach and that she thought she was okay and that probably if she and Betsy went and had lunch and then—when they came back—if they all went down to the playroom and started planning the Easter egg hunt with the playroom lady, she'd be fine.

29

At three, Betsy and his mother returned with yellow and purple crepe paper and bags of green cellophane grass to stuff in the Easter baskets that the playroom lady had bought. His mother seemed better. At the meeting in the playroom, it was decided that if it was a nice day, they would take all the kids—there were currently only six on the Acute Ward and eight on the Reconstruction—up on the elevator to the patio on the roof where they would have the egg hunt, but if the weather was bad, Betsy and his mother and the playroom lady would hide the eggs and candy in the playroom.

But the next morning was beautiful. The sky is blue, Betsy kept saying when she came in. A really *blue* blue, a New Mexico blue sky—it's going to be a wonderful day. She'd made cinnamon buns and brought them all wrapped up in tinfoil. Riley's mother went upstairs to help the playroom lady hide the candy. Betsy sat down and continued on with the reading of the Hardy Boys mystery and their adventures out west, though the only thing Melvin wanted to do was go find the candy. He kept fidgeting. You'll have to wait, Betsy said, until all the candy gets hidden.

And then it was time. The kids who could walk raced for the elevator. They had to be herded back into the room, though, until one of the nurses was ready to go with them. And then they couldn't look for candy until the kids in wheelchairs or on gurneys arrived, so it was another impatient wait outside the patio.

Riley's graft was too fresh, so he couldn't walk. He was propped up on pillows, sitting high on a gurney, all wrapped in a sheet and looking a little like an Indian chief.

He couldn't get down and look for eggs and candy.

For just one small minute, he wished with all his heart he could hunt for candy, but suddenly he realized he was outside. The air smelled so good! He could smell the water. He wondered how close the ocean was. He wanted to see the waves and the sand, the little sandpipers and sea gulls his mother had been telling him about. He wanted to walk on the Seawall.

Riley hadn't been outside for nearly three months. In fact, he'd forgotten that the outside existed. All he'd thought about for the longest time was the hospital, the doctors and the nurses, himself and the surgeries, the new kids and the old kids and how they all got there—not a thing else. But now he only wanted to get out—he was nearly dizzy with impatience. He wanted to walk around Galveston first—but not for long—and immediately after that, he wanted to go home. He wanted to get back to his house and his father, he wanted to get back to school, he wanted to see Greg and to tell Jason and Sarah that he was back and that Greg was his best friend and that they should bug off.

JUST BEFORE HE WENT to bed that Easter Sunday night, Riley counted with pleasure the events of the last week—

1. Melvin Pitts suddenly becoming a boy Riley could talk to—
2. The Easter egg hunt and the intoxicating smell of the outside—
3. Betsy's wonderful visit and his mother's contentment—
4. (and then re-counted—again!)—the time he'd spent with Eddie and his sisters in the playroom.

And then he dreamed of home.

30

But on Monday morning, the tub men said *Uh oh* and took Riley right back upstairs without putting him in the tub and left him sitting on the gurney in the middle of Room 312 and the doctors and the nurses came flooding in from the nurse's station and stood around him, pushing and poking at his back, going over every inch of his much-too-naked body, especially the right side of his face. One of the nurses started shutting the blinds, always a bad sign.

He could hear his mother's laughter as she came down and around the hall, talking to her best friend Betsy. And then she came in the room, looking so flushed and happy and for all intents and purposes like she expected for him to be sitting on the end of his bed with his suitcase packed beside him and all ready to go back home—and like all these people were in the room celebrating the fact that he was completely healed.

It took her a minute—maybe more—to take in what was happening: everyone was there—yes—and they were all staring at the graft on his back, or rather the place on his back where the graft should have been, but wasn't. Dr. Walker—so tall and serious—put his hand on his mother's shoulder—she looked tiny beside him—while he told her that the new graft had fallen off Riley's back—her face went white and she had to sit down—and also that Riley had contracted a staph infection on the right side of his face. The sloughed graft meant another surgery on his back, and the staph infection meant being hooked up again to more IVs. And both things together meant that they would be in the hospital at a bare minimum ten more days. Betsy kept offering to stay and saying that she could call her work and take more time off, that she could cancel her one o'clock flight out of Houston. He knew his mother wanted her to stay, Riley could tell, but she wouldn't say it, she'd lost her bearings, she couldn't take it all in—and so, an hour later, she was all alone by herself sitting beside his bed, her arms folded up on her chest and her lips all tight and stuck together, just as unhappy as if her best friend had never been here and she had never had the chance to tell her everything.

He lay in bed and cried. He didn't even care that Melvin and Carnell could hear him. He hated Dr. Walker.

He hated the nurses. He hated the graft that fell off and he hated the new one they were going to put on. And he didn't want to hear another word about fire—his fire or anyone else's. He hated fire, and he wanted to be out of this horrible hospital more than anything else in the whole world.

HE HAD ANOTHER SURGERY the next morning, early—same nightmare. And then three or four days of absolutely forlorn recovery—IVs in his arm, propped up on his side—during which he kept himself steadfastly focused on the TV. He didn't care what was on, only that it was on. He didn't care that Carnell wanted to talk—he wouldn't answer—or that Melvin kept telling him to get up and go down with him to the playroom—he wasn't moving—or that the nurses weren't letting him out of their sight. He and his mother remained faithfully at their posts—he in his bed, she in her chair, not talking to anyone. His mother leaked tears and didn't even try to hide them.

Even when Mr. Loflin brought news that there was a new girl from Tupelo on the Acute Ward—*in pretty bad shape*—the kind of news that was truly the most interesting—and that Pat had started to eat by herself and actually walked to the bathroom, he didn't respond.

His mother tried to be polite, smiling as if she wanted to hear more.

Yessiree, said Mr. Loflin. Miss Washington made a little old bracelet for Pat's wrist that holds a little spoon and she made that mean girl start picking up Cheetos with that same spoon. Pat said she couldn't do it.

Stick them Cheetos in your mouth, you silly girl, said Miss Washington.

I wants a prize, Mr. Loflin screeched in imitation of Pat. *Where's my prize?*

Them Cheetos are your prize, said Miss Washington. Keep eating them.

According to Mr. Loflin, Miss Washington made Pat stand up, too, and start trying to walk. Only the first time Pat tried it, she threw up. Miss Washington just kept pushing her, until she was getting up and walking along two poles and she was putting all the Cheetos in her mouth. All by herself.

And then I tell her, girl, I hear you can eat all by yourself.

I needs help, she yells back at me.

Not from me, I tell her.

She cried, oh, how she cried, but she ate everything on her plate. So then I told all the nurses, *Lookee here, would you?* And we all came in to look at her and she started yelling at us but she was laughing, too. First time I seen that mean girl laugh! I brought her a cup of ice cream for dessert and she ate that, too, all by herself!

So, Miss Martin, Mr. Loflin concluded, it won't be too long before that mean girl moves into Room 312. Are you ready for her?

31

The next Monday, Dr. Walker told his mother that the graft on Riley's back had taken and that almost all of the open spots on his body had healed. That information had the same power as the Prince's kiss in *Sleeping Beauty*, for, with that news, his mother—just like Sleeping Beauty—seemed to rise up out of a deep sleep. Even though the doctor said they still had to wait another week for the antibiotics to clear up his staph infection, she began to make plans to go home and she said she thought she'd go buy herself a new blouse or maybe even a dress and she suggested that, right after lunch, they go down to the playroom, even though Riley, because of the graft on his back, really couldn't get up and exactly play. But maybe he could color, she suggested, or do a puzzle. Or just sit there. She didn't care—it was time for a change.

The playroom was close to empty, except for a big, fat old lady and two very skinny, very white people who sat on either side of her. The three of them looked up at Riley and his mother as soon as she wheeled him into the playroom, watching them as they crossed the room, their mouths open. It made his mother nervous, he could tell, because she stuck out her hand toward them right away and said her name was Cynthia Martin and that this was her son, Riley. The old woman, who wore pink bedroom slippers and a too-short dress stretched tight across her knees, ignored his mother's hand and started talking, just as if she'd been waiting for hours for Riley and his mother to come.

She said she was from Tupelo. His mother countered by saying quickly that she was from El Paso, but that she had been born in New Jersey. NEW JERSEY, his mother said slowly as if the three of them were hard of hearing. While she was laying out this important piece of information, she tried to find herself a chair to sit in, one far enough away so she and Riley could avoid the woman from Tupelo and her pale companions, but she didn't succeed. Nothing was far enough away once the old lady started talking.

She said that she was here because of her granddaughter. That was her opening line. Then she began in earnest, laboring through the details of her granddaughter's ordeal in a drawl as flat and indifferent as if she were talking about the offspring of some Chinaman who lived in the furthest reaches of Mongolia and not her very own flesh and blood. The minute her story began, Riley and his mother were stuck, as surely as if the curtain had risen on a hair-raising play and someone had strapped them in their seats. The old woman had an umbrella in her left hand, a black, dirty-looking thing with a torn ruffle, and she used that to tap on the low table next to her when she mentioned anything that was particularly gruesome.

During the fat lady's recital, the man and woman on either side of her didn't say a word. Their faces were whiter than any faces Riley had ever seen. Both of them were preoccupied with chewing gum, popping and cracking it at the most unexpected times, and both of them were staring at Riley. Riley stared right back, as fascinated with them as they were with him. The three of them, he noted, smelled terrible, like cigarettes and old tuna fish and greasy French fries. In this regard, he noticed that his mother kept her face all squeezed up, as if she were trying not to breathe.

I went to town, was how the fat lady launched into her story. It being the first of the month and her daughter eligible for welfare and food stamps.

She had to go. Couldn't trust them to go alone, she said, squinting narrowly at Riley's mother as if shutting the white, skinny couple out of her vision would also keep them from hearing her. The boyfriend was no good. Had been in jail twice and couldn't be trusted with money. Her own daughter didn't have no sense. The things she could tell. Tap, tap, tap went her umbrella on the low table.

The old woman sighed—a bit of spit suddenly appearing on the side of her mouth as she did so—and continued. They left the granddaughter at home alone. She was seven. *Plenty big enough to be left alone. Plenty big enough to know how to cook. Big enough to know how to turn on the oven by herself.*

Anyways she was sick with a fever and the chills. She stayed in bed. She had on her pink nightgown, the one they give her for her birthday, from the Kmart.

They had them this lady next door. A nigra woman with a big mouth. This nigra woman had a big black buck who come and beat her up a few nights a week. Tap. Tap. Tap.

They both was in the house next door at the same time that the granddaughter stood up to try to warm herself from the chills in front of the oven in her pink nightgown.

Riley's mother scowled and shifted in her seat, as if she couldn't quite see the relationship between these two events.

The Tupelo lady said that it would be a matter for the police to be investigating. As soon as them doctors found out for sure whether the girl would live or die they were going to look her over to see if that black buck had touched her. Tap. Tap. Tap. Because from what the nigra lady said, it had been the black buck who first seen her come out on the front porch of their house, spinning and screaming and all on fire. That's what the nigra with the big mouth told the police. But there weren't no black buck around anywhere by the time the Tupelo lady got home with her daughter and her daughter's worthless boyfriend and the four sacks full of groceries. And the granddaughter couldn't tell them nothing. She was half burnt to death.

The lady from Tupelo wiped her mouth off with a dirty piece of Kleenex she held tight in her hand.

The nigra next door was the stupidest nigra the Tupelo lady had ever met. When her and her daughter and the daughter's worthless boyfriend had come back from town, the nigra could hardly tell them what had happened or where the granddaughter had gone or why the house smelled like smoke.

She's gone, the Tupelo lady whined, imitating her stupid neighbor. *Your girl is gone.*

Where's she gone? they demanded of her.

Don't know, the nigra had wailed. Didn't tell me, but she gone. Gone in the am-bu-lance.

They called the police and the police finally came and took them to the hospital. They had the si-reen on. The umbrella struck the floor while the fat lady from Tupelo raised her neck and howled to demonstrate the truth of that very fact.

There was a bunch of doctors. One after another. There was a little-bitty doctor who had no hair on his head and he said the granddaughter was burnt inside and out.

There was one who was a Jap and he said she was going to die that day. Said she was burnt thirty-six.

There was one even who was a nigra. A fe-male! And she said they were gong to have to fly the girl to the charitable hospital for burns in Galveston, Texas, in whose stuffy third-floor playroom they now all sat.

They didn't fly the girl that same day, though. Mostly what they did was to keep them all sitting there in that hospital in Tupelo way past suppertime. And they were getting tired, too. The grandmother got a hold of the Jap and told him about being so hungry and so tired and having nothing but food stamps for money and he took them down to the cafeteria and bought them some supper.

She didn't care what they said about Japs.

Fried chicken and lady peas and mashed potatoes and black bottom pie for dessert. And then he called the police and they came and drove them home. And hardly before they even got to sleep, the police car came back to get them and take them to the airport. Dark it was and still nighttime and them with just the clothes they had on and a change of underwear and a couple of sandwiches in a paper sack. And the 'frigerator back in Tupelo full of food from the food stamps and them not having any idea how long all this would take.

A private jet flew them all down to Galveston. The granddaughter had a nurse. The girl was wrapped in white bandages all over. All over her hands and her legs and her head and her face. And she smelled. Lord. Gawd. The whole airplane was filled with her smell.

The umbrella clattered to the floor. The lady from Tupelo shut her eyes and stopped talking as abruptly as she had started.

Riley sat up straight. He thought the Tupelo lady's story was about to end and that his mother would get up and leave, but the story had, apparently, only just begun.

32

Riley's mother tapped her faded red sandals impatiently on the floor, something she used to do when Miss MacGwyn would get going and wouldn't stop. She shook her head and pushed back her hair and then looked over at the clock on the wall. Riley looked, too. Only ten minutes had passed though it seemed like forever. He tried to roll his eyes at her to suggest maybe they should leave, but she didn't seem to be paying attention.

She just stared at the strange group sitting across from them—as if she was going to sit there until they told her she could go. The grandmother looked like she had fallen asleep. That was fine with Riley. He really didn't want to hear any more about that fat lady's granddaughter. He was normally intensely interested in all the new cases that came into the hospital; he had actually heard Mr. Loflin mention the fat lady's granddaughter, but it was one thing to hear about her from the tub men and from

Mr. Loflin and a whole other thing to hear about her from this awful lady—just looking at her made his stomach queasy.

Suddenly the grandmother's eyes popped open and she began again. She smelt like burnt meat, she said. That whole airplane smelt like burnt meat. I got sick, couldn't hardly stand it. Later I seen her chest, looks like a slab of raw beef. She got fire on her face, too. Doctor says she going to have scars all over her. Ain't no man ever going to want to touch her, that's one thing.

His mother looked away quickly, out the window. It seemed to Riley that she had disappeared—for all intents and purposes, she was no longer there.

The fat lady seemed to have noticed the change, too, because she leaned forward and asked pointedly, What's the number of your kid?

His mother frowned, but didn't respond.

What's his number? said the lady from Tupelo again, pointing at Riley. He started to answer himself—after all, he knew all the answers, too, probably better than his mother—but his mother stopped him with a hand to his knee.

Yes, she said. She folded her arms across her chest and tapped her red sandal on the floor. It seemed a long time before she actually answered. She was mad, Riley could tell—she was talking very carefully and very very quietly as if she was afraid of what she was going to say.

Do you mean what room is he in or what percent of his body was burned? That's what you mean, don't you? It's called the percentage. What percentage of his body was burned, is that what you want to know?

The lady from Tupelo blinked.

My son, continued his mother, was burned over sixty-three percent of his body.

Yeah? said the lady from Tupelo. My granddaughter got seventy.

His mother's sandal hit the floor. I thought you said it was thirty-six percent, she said.

Yeah, said the Tupelo lady.

Well, what is it? Is it thirty-six percent or seventy percent? Because there's a big difference. His mother sat up very straight in her chair. Is it all third-degree?

It's bad, said the Tupelo lady.

His mother fussed with the creases in her pants, pushing at them nervously with her hand. Her ankle wiggled of its own accord.

My son is burned almost entirely third-degree, she said suddenly, the words exploding from her. She glowered at the lady from Tupelo, trying to hold that person's watery eyes with her own, but the lady from Tupelo looked right past her. That's the maximum amount of burn there can be, she pushed on, but deliberately now, precisely. That's all three layers of skin. Sixty-three percent. Now that's bad.

Yeah? said the lady from Tupelo. She shut her eyes.

He is burned on the top of his head, continued Riley's mother, on every bit of his face, on his left arm, on his back, and on his chest. He lost his ears and his nose and three fingers.

The Tupelo lady's head slipped forward a little, as if she were just catching herself from falling asleep.

He's bad, said his mother. Riley was afraid she was going to start crying. He prayed with all his might that she wouldn't—she was hardly reliable anymore in that regard—especially in front of this horrible fat lady.

Sixty-three percent, all third-degree, is bad, she said again to whoever she thought might be listening. He's been in the hospital for three months. For over three months. And I've been here with him the whole time. I had to leave my whole world behind me.

No one seemed interested. The daughter's worthless boyfriend put his hand in his breast pocket and took out another stick of gum in a motion so slow that Riley's mother was arrested by it. When he finally crinkled open the silver foil, she shook, it surprised her so, and she jumped and pushed ahead, now fully irritated. Riley thought her voice was just a little too loud.

I went in to see him right away, right after the fire, long before they flew him here in the private plane, she said. My husband—she said it emphatically, as if the word might have no meaning to her audience—was with me that whole first week. Then he had to go back to work. We just could not afford to have him out of work for more than a month. He works, she said slowly. In El Paso.

When I first saw my son, his skin was falling off in strips and it was yellow. And when they took him into the tubs to take the skin off, I could hear him screaming. Now—he was one they thought would die. He was bad.

Riley's mother took a long, deep breath. She rubbed her face with both her hands.

But your granddaughter, she said finally, if she is indeed burned over thirty-six percent of her body, is going to be fine. Thirty-six percent is nothing.

But the fat lady and her daughter and her daughter's worthless boyfriend didn't seem to care. The two of them kept right on chewing gum. The fat lady twisted and turned the Kleenex she held clutched in her hand.

• • •

Riley's mother leaned her chin on her hand and shut her eyes. And dozed off, or must have. Because when the Tupelo lady spoke next, his mother jumped, like she'd been sound asleep.

What's his name? she said, leaning forward toward his mother. She didn't ask Riley, didn't even look at him. But he didn't feel like answering anyway.

His name is Riley, said his mother. Didn't I already tell you?

Yeah? said the lady from Tupelo. She dabbed at her lip with the rumpled Kleenex. Why's he wear that thing over his face?

His mother sat up straight. That's a mask, she said. All the children wear masks if they are burned on their faces. Haven't you seen any of the other children wearing masks?

The lady from Tupelo sniffled.

Well, said his mother, the masks are a major breakthrough in burn care. A very major breakthrough.

The Tupelo lady looked at her sullenly.

Your granddaughter will have to wear a mask, said his mother. She tightened her lips. She looked very serious. Just like my son. Just like everyone else.

That so? said the lady from Tupelo. She crossed her

arms up over her chest. She didn't say anything at all. And then, suddenly, How'd he get burned?

Riley's mother sat back in her chair. He was in a garage fire, she said. It was nobody's fault, it was an accident.

My girl wasn't playing with no matches, said the Tupelo lady. She knows how to light the stove.

Well, said Riley's mother. My boy doesn't play with matches either.

The two women stared at each other.

Riley wasn't sure why his mother had lied. But he knew she wasn't happy. She scowled at the Tupelo lady's pink bedroom slippers. That lady's toenails were yellow and dirty and long.

The Tupelo lady sighed, an enormous sawing noise. I got a bad heart, she said. Had a heart attack last year.

His mother's red sandal slapped against her foot.

My girl here can't work. She's got to take care of her kid. They're giving us a room in the Holiday Inn and giving me and the girl seven dollars a day for food. They got king-size beds over there and a twenty-four-inch color TV. Don't know what they're going to do about *him*. Said they couldn't pay for more than me and the girl because we're kinfolks. He's not the kid's father.

Well! said his mother.

And with that word, she stood up. We've got to go, she said. She took Riley's wheelchair and maneuvered it in the direction of the door, then stood there awhile—Riley could almost hear her thinking—he knew what she was like—she felt guilty, he knew it—then turned slowly back.

Well, she said again, I'm sorry. And she pushed the wheelchair some more.

Then turned around again. I think your daughter, your granddaughter, will be fine. I think that the first couple of weeks are the worst, she went on. I remember that my first couple of weeks here were the worst I've ever spent in my whole life. I didn't know if Riley would live or die. But it gets better.

Riley shifted around in his chair impatiently.

Just hold on, she said to Riley, and then turned back to the people from Tupelo. Let me qualify that. It gets better until you realize that your child will . . . have scars. Her voice got lower. Now that is really the worst part. But even that gets better. You come to terms with it. You accept it. You get a handle on it and after a while it hardly bothers you anymore.

The trio from Tupelo listened to this extraordinary capsulization of his mother's experience without showing any sign whatsoever of having heard or understood it. Riley could see that she was waiting for them to comment, but they didn't say a word.

She stood watching them for a minute. Well, okay, she said finally and then turned and pushed Riley along the hall. Midway through, just about at the point where the smell of strawberry milk was overwhelming, she started to blow air out through her mouth, as if she'd just run a long race and hadn't gotten to the finish line.

33

On Tuesday morning early, even before his mother arrived and even before Riley or Carnell or Melvin were awake, Pat came into Room 312—on her own two feet—and sat down on Parker's bed. She had all her worldly belongings in a drawstring bag.

I eats by myself. And I can walk, she announced to the sleeping room. And I don't pee in my bed.

Melvin had a fit. He told Mr. Loflin and everyone who would listen, including the doctor, just what he thought. *She's a girl. And she's a nigger!* he fussed. But Mr. Loflin said that they had promised Pat she could come in to Room 312 if she learned to eat and walk and stopped peeing in her bed. And Pat had done all those things. And she'd even started to laugh. So that's what they were doing and Melvin was just going to have to live with it.

Pat just sat on Parker's old bed, not letting anything Melvin say get to her, acting like she was deaf. Carnell being Carnell, he came over and sat beside her.

Riley thought it was a little odd to have a girl in Room 312, but he didn't really care one way or the other about Pat because he was leaving soon, probably by the end of the week. He wasn't going to say anything to her anyway. He wasn't going to let anything bother him. And nothing seemed to bother his mother, either, for when she came in and saw Pat on Parker's bed, she went right over and told her hi. Mr. Loflin came in when he saw Riley's mother and the two of them made a big to-do over Pat and her recent accomplishments. Now, said Mr. Loflin on his way out, you be nice or you won't get to stay in this room with Miss Martin.

And you be nice, too, Melvin, hear?

Riley's mother helped Pat put her things in the nightstand beside her bed. Pat put the old black plastic comb that Betsy had given her—her prized possession—on top of the nightstand. And then she dragged a chair over next to Riley's mother, and sat down, staking her claim.

Pat wondered right away if she could come live with them.

• • •

ON WEDNESDAY MORNING—just like the answer to a prayer Riley had never even prayed—Dr. Walker came into Room 312 with Marilyn Hooper—the lady who had been burned herself—and with Melinda Kepler, the social worker—a short blond lady his mother didn't seem to like too much—and told his mother that the three of them had been talking and that they all felt that she needed to take Riley out on an afternoon pass sometime soon, like the next day or Friday.

A pass? his mother said. The color rushed out of her face. A pass? What's that mean?

A pass, said Melinda Kepler. A chance to get out of the hospital, a chance to take Riley out before you actually go home. *So he can get used to being out in public.*

Get him used to being out in public? his mother repeated. Why would I want to do that? I'll have plenty of time to be out in public next week when we go back to El Paso.

Well, said the social worker, it would be appropriate for you to take him out in public now, *before* you return to El Paso. You don't know anyone here in Galveston. Being out among people you don't know will . . . will be critical . . . for Riley's success. And besides, she said with a big smile, it will do the two of you a world of good.

His mother flexed her hands in and out like she was trying to get extra air to come in through her fingers. Then she jammed her fists into her eyes.

Oh please don't cry . . .

Listen, she said to Marilyn Hooper, her voice unsteady, doesn't the hospital have a car I can use?

A car? the social worker interrupted. Oh no, a car won't do.

Why not?

A car won't accomplish anything.

His mother peered at Melinda Kepler. *What am I trying to accomplish?*

You need to be out among people, not inside a car. Don't you see?

Apparently she didn't see because she sat down in her chair and didn't talk for the rest of the morning while Riley bragged to the other kids about everything that he and his mother would do on *his* pass. Of course, Melvin and Pat and Carnell wanted to go, too, but Riley just ignored them—after all, Dr. Walker and the psychiatrist and the social worker had come to *his* mother, not theirs. *Okay, so, they didn't have mothers, at least not here—*

First, he said, they would go to the Baskin-Robbins for an ice-cream sundae and then they would go see the ocean and the waves that people had been telling him about and he and his mother could sit on a bench like she used to do with her auntie and her mother and she could tell him stories about Lavallette and then they could walk along the Seawall where, he'd heard, lots of kids roller-skated and rode bikes and then they would go see his mother's apartment and just before they came back to the hospital, he would get a hamburger at Rusty's, where his mother had told him she often ate dinner. He wanted to see it all! He couldn't wait to be outside.

BUT IT WASN'T UNTIL Friday afternoon that his mother got around to actually taking him, and he knew that she wouldn't have even done that except that Riley reminded her every few minutes about the places they would go on his pass and that Dr. Walker had ordered it and that she had to do what Dr. Walker told her to do. He couldn't figure out why the whole thing made her so sad, or why she didn't seem happy to be taking him out to look around town—it was the most exciting thing that had happened to him in months, except for meeting Eddie—couldn't she see that?—and he was desperate to get outside—he needed it!—it would do him a world of good!—or why she kept telling him he couldn't go because he didn't have the right clothes or shoes even and that they didn't have money to buy any and that she herself didn't have a decent dress, even though she never wore a dress hardly ever, let alone at the hospital—no one wore dresses at the hospital, except maybe Miss MacGwyn—or why she said they couldn't go to any of the places he kept telling her about, but only to her apartment.

He told her he didn't need new clothes. He told her to call Dad and have him send his Levis and his favorite shirt from home.

But she didn't seem to be listening.

34

Riley had the terrible, horrible, sinking feeling that his mother was just going to ignore the doctors completely. She stayed home on Thursday afternoon. She didn't show up on Friday morning. He thought about telling the nurses to tell Dr. Walker, so he could send the social worker and Marilyn Hooper out to Mrs. Griswald's to bring his mother in and force her to take him on his pass. He was madder at her than he'd ever been in his whole life and he sat up in his bed pouting, feeling certain that she was going to shame him in front of his roommates—and worse, deny him the chance to go out on *his* pass and see all the wonderful places he had planned to see.

But, to his surprise and astonishment, right at one o'clock on Friday, when the morning visiting hours were over and the other kids were down at the playroom, his mother appeared at the door of Room 312.

She was wearing a dress. It was a purple sundress. It had little narrow straps so that her shoulders were bare—and very white—and a skirt that came to her knees. She had bare legs—also white—and new shoes, white sandals with little pieces of purple and pink glass stuck in them and she was wearing pink lipstick—the sight of her startled Riley almost as much as Eddie Rabedeaux's face had weeks before.

She had shopping bags in both hands and a new purple purse slung over one shoulder. And her face told him that if he said so much as boo to her, she would fly right out of the room and never come back.

She walked quickly across to his bed, putting her bags and purse down. She spoke to Riley in a whisper, even though they were alone—maybe it was because it was officially nap time or because all the lights were dimmed all over the Acute Ward. If he looked out of his window into the nursing station, he could see younger children sleeping in their beds and in their cribs, shrouded in white sheets. In one room, white curtains surrounded a single bed. The room was dark and the nurses and Dr. Walker were going in and coming out. Mr. Loflin said it was the Tupelo lady's granddaughter. Maybe she was going to die.

Here is a new shirt, his mother said very fast. She

pushed it into his hands without looking at him. I just went to the department store in the mall and bought it this morning. That's where I've been for the last two days. Green and blue check. You always like green and blue.

A new shirt! he blinked. Wasn't Dad going to mail one over here? He tried not to raise his voice.

Look, she said sharply. Don't start that. Your father wouldn't have had time to mail it.

He stood stiffly while she pushed his arms into the sleeves. Those stupid people from Tupelo are sitting out in the hall, she said. Don't they have anywhere to go? She looked up across the hall at the room with the white curtains. Oh geez, maybe that old lady's granddaughter's not doing so well. She pushed the hair off her face. Well . . . you're going to look nice when you walk past them, no matter what's going on.

It's too small, he whimpered.

No, she said. It's just right. And here are the pants.

They were dress pants, made of polyester. This blue will pick up the blue in your shirt, she said, as if he cared.

He groaned. Couldn't you have asked Dad just to mail my old jeans?

I told you already about your father. You have gotten fatter with all that milk they're making you drink, she said firmly. You wouldn't be able to wear your old jeans even if your father had sent them. Now stand up.

Why didn't you buy me some new jeans then?

These are just like new jeans, she said, touching his leg so he would raise it.

New jeans! he sputtered. These are like something you go to church in.

Well, she said, pursing her mouth together. This is a special occasion. Like going to church, she added grimly. And you're going to look nice if it kills us. Now sit down while I put your socks and shoes on.

The socks were dress socks, and the shoes were brown. He had wanted sneakers and gray athletic socks, and they argued again. He cried until the eyes of his mask were wet.

They hurt, he whispered.

Of course they don't hurt. I matched them up exactly against the picture I drew of your foot, she said, although that wasn't exactly true. She had matched them up exactly against the picture but she hadn't even considered the Ace bandages that were wrapped under his feet, and all up his legs.

The socks are too hot.

She hadn't thought about the socks either.

Listen to me, she said. She grabbed his shoulders. Do

you want to go out on this—this pass? Because I don't. Not at all. But if you want to do it, we're going to do it right. So make up your mind this minute.

She went right on talking even though he knew exactly what he was going to do—*go out on this pass if it killed him.* Your shoes fit and so do your socks. You're acting like a spoiled brat.

Yes, everything fits: the socks, the shoes, the pants, the shirt.

She walked around the room gathering up her purse, putting away the boxes and paper sacks. She went into the bathroom to wash her hands. When she came out, he was standing up, ready to go.

You're ready? Okay, let's go then. And don't push me anymore, hear? I've already spent all this money on . . . everything, money we didn't even have. And this dress—God almighty. I can't believe I bought this dress.

Riley couldn't believe it either, but he wasn't going to say another word. She kept right on talking. *What was I thinking? I look like Corliss MacGwyn. Only I'm not Corliss MacGwyn. I must be a fool.*

They walked out into the bright, sunlit hallway, his mother's hand pressing against his shoulder—and it was there that he heard the flat, lifeless drawl of the lady from Tupelo once more. Riley remembered her and the vacant gum-chewing pair as if he had met them many years ago in a dream.

It was apparent that his mother—even though she had just seen them—had forgotten them, too. Oh, God, she said, those people. She pressed her nails into Riley's arm so hard that he winced.

Take a deep breath, she said. Don't say a word. I'll do all the talking.

WHY THEY COULDN'T JUST walk past the people from Tupelo, he didn't know, but he didn't dare suggest it.

Then they were there in the waiting corridor, standing right in front of the fat lady—on either side her daughter and her daughter's worthless boyfriend. It was hot—no air-conditioning in the halls. The sun outside the thin hospital window was pitched almost directly overhead, hard and yellow. The narrow corridor baked in its glare and there was—once more—that heavy smell of greasy French fries and cigarettes—and something else that didn't smell good at all.

Hello again, his mother said, much too cheerfully for Riley's comfort. She cleared her throat. Here I am again. And here's Riley. She put her arm around him. We're getting ready to go out on an afternoon pass.

The people from Tupelo leaned back away from them. Not all at once. Not quickly. But ever so slowly. And their eyes grew bigger the further away they got.

Here he is, his mother said again. This is Riley. She gave her head a quick, hard shake. You already saw him the other day, don't you remember?

The fat lady didn't answer. She kept squeezing and turning the dirty Kleenex in her hand.

You going to let him go out with that thing on? she said suddenly. He looks like a bank robber.

His mother winced. This is his mask. Don't you remember that I was telling you about it?

Their eyes roamed freely over every inch of Riley's body, from the top of the brown hood to the flat, red emptiness of his missing ears to the piece of matted hair that stuck out from behind the mask to the splints and Ace wraps that covered his hands, down over all his new clothes.

The fat lady sucked in hard.

Gawd, she said.

The worthless boyfriend leaned over and mumbled something to the fat lady.

Riley's mother peered at him. What did he say? she asked the grandmother.

He wants to know what happened to your kid, she said.

His mother screwed up her face in disbelief. What? she said.

He wants to know what happened to your kid, the fat lady repeated.

What do you mean? his mother said. He was burned! Everyone in the hospital was burned! Your granddaughter was burned! She's going to look just . . . just like . . .

Riley was tugging at her skirt, wanting to go on. His mother shouldn't say anything about the Tupelo lady's granddaughter because, right at this minute, it didn't seem like she was doing very well.

Just you wait a minute, she said, pushing Riley's hand away from her. Just wait a minute, she said. Everybody just wait a minute. She put a strong hand on his shoulder and took a deep breath. I have to say something, she said to him, so you'll just have to wait a minute.

She turned to face the family from Tupelo, but even her anger could not force them to look at her. They still stared at Riley.

You don't seem to realize what this boy has been through. She pushed her hair back off her face. He's been burned. He almost died. I mean, you haven't seen half of these kids here. Some of them don't even have noses. Some of them have lost their ears. They're blind. And they can't hear. They can fix . . . they can do plastic surgery.

Mom, Riley mouthed.

Your granddaughter's going to . . . she's going to be . . . , she said, her voice beginning to break.

It was no use. The people from Tupelo sat with their mouths open and kept right on staring at Riley while the hot Galveston sun glared through the window with equal lack of sympathy on all of them.

Lord have mercy, said the lady from Tupelo.

The worthless boyfriend leaned over again to talk to the fat lady. She mumbled a reply and he answered and the fat lady's daughter acquiesced with a nod. The fat lady from Tupelo turned in their direction. He says you need something to cover yourself with, she said.

What? said Riley's mother.

Yeah, said the fat lady. You can't go out there without something to cover you. Why, you only got those little straps over your shoulders.

Riley could feel his mother tighten up.

It's going to be hot, the fat lady declared. It's going to be hotter here than it ever was in New Jersey. And anyway, I always cover myself, the fat lady went on. Keeps me from the sun.

There was a leaning forward of the fat lady's daughter, then a shuffling around with her hand on the floor. She brought up the ragged black taffeta umbrella, the one the fat lady had used to punctuate all her statements the other day in the playroom. She handed it over her mother's stomach to the outstretched hand of the worthless boyfriend and then he pushed it up its handle until it opened, limp and spokeless in places, but still serviceable. He passed it back to his girlfriend's mother and she took it and held it out toward Riley and his mother.

This'll cover you good, said the fat lady, almost tenderly. It'll cover both you and him.

Riley's mother blinked. I can't take that from you, she said.

Well, you better, said the fat lady. We're the only ones here that got one.

His mother didn't move. Riley couldn't imagine her even touching the umbrella, let alone carrying it, especially now when she had bought herself a new dress. She would look like a circus clown with the fat lady's black umbrella.

His mother and the fat lady would have hung suspended there a long time, held by the one's insistence to give and the other's inability to accept the gift, only Riley decided to step forward—he was eager, after all, to be on his way—and took the ragged covering from the Tupelo lady. Thank you, he said carefully.

He pulled at his mother's hand to indicate that it was

time they should set out and she obeyed, letting him lead her out and away from the narrow waiting corridor, away from the fat lady from Tupelo and her daughter and the daughter's worthless boyfriend.

He brought her down to wait at the end of the hall in front of the elevator, even though he knew that she never took the elevator if she could help it.

35

Riley Martin and his mother got in the elevator, but she right away pushed the button for the second floor.

What are you doing? Riley wanted to know, but she didn't answer.

They got off there and went down the stairwell where she stuck the fat lady's umbrella on a window ledge.

Someone will find it, Mom, Riley protested.

No one but me ever walks the stairs, I promise, she said. We'll get it on the way back and give it to them. They walked down to the lobby. *I can't believe she gave it to me!*

Over by the hospital were the busiest streets, the most people. Riley was ready to be out in them—letting everyone know that he was on a pass and that today was his first day out of the hospital in three months—but his mother stood peering through the big glass door with a scowl on her face, considering the landscape and its inhabitants as if she were about to change her mind completely.

Come on, Mom, he said. You don't want to run into that fat lady again, do you?

That thought seemed to get her started. She cleared her throat, but right then the automatic sliding doors to the drug store in the bank building across the street opened up and a group of women suddenly appeared. They made Riley think of—Miss MacGwyn—all dressed up in hats and dresses and high heels. With what his mother had on right then, she could have been one of them. The women stood a minute, turning and talking and laughing—one with her hand on her head to hold her straw hat in place gestured over toward the hospital and they continued on, heading right toward Riley and his mother.

Ohhhh, Jesus, she said suddenly. *Charity ladies.* She breathed in deeply. *You're pushing me, sir*, she said, just as if Jesus himself was there with them—she must really be losing it, Riley thought. *I don't have much rope to play with,* she hissed.

She jerked Riley by the hand. *We're going out the other door.* She pulled him down past the elevators and out the side entrance toward the parking lot.

They inched along—truly it was hard to walk fast, let alone walk, when your feet and legs were wrapped in ace bandages. He was dying for some ice cream from Baskin-Robbins—but he didn't want to say anything that would make her change her mind. Not a word about how hot *it* was or how hot *he* was—it was two in the afternoon, the very hottest part of the day anywhere near any ocean in the whole world—you could have taken a bath in the sticking salt water that filled the air—because he knew that if he complained even once she'd turn around and take him right back to his room. And that would be the end of that, doctor's orders or no doctor's orders.

So he just let her drag him along—it was *really really* hard to walk—letting the intoxicating smell of the ocean and the sand and the wild cawing of the sea gulls and some big black birds flapping through the tall, dark trees and the promise of Rocky Road ice cream in his mouth distract and steady him enough so that he wouldn't faint. He just couldn't faint. His mother would kill him.

Can't you walk any faster? she snapped. You've been lying in bed now for three months. You ought to be strong by now. I don't want to just creep along. She pushed her hair back from her face. I'm sweating like a pig, she added. *Oh Lord, listen to me.*

I can't, Mom, Riley fussed, his voice muffled by the brown hood and the white plastic life mask the hood held in place. It's hard to walk in these shoes. I'm tired.

You're tired, I'm tired, I'm so tired, she chanted as she pulled him along. Three months of sitting by your damn bed. I'm so sick of this place. I want to go home!

I want to go home, too, Riley cried in agreement. I want to see Dad.

Oh you! You always want what you can't have. Always always always always! Just quit it, would you? They turned a corner.

He's working, your father is, his mother said suddenly. For absolutely nothing. Making no money, not getting anywhere, isn't handy—has a hammer and a Phillips screwdriver thrown in the bottom of a drawer in the kitchen!—the screen door is falling off, the windows don't go up and down, that stinking old house. Can't make enough money to fix it! Well, just how come we don't have the money? What's our problem? We went to college, didn't we? How come everybody else is making it except us?

OUT OF A SIDE STREET a man appeared—a hospital person—a doctor or a resident or an intern or a student—in a long white coat. He was tall and very black. Riley's mother slowed down, stood completely still, and crossed both arms up high in front of her chest.

Don't say a word, she hissed at Riley out of the side of her mouth. Stop your fussing, right now! She looked up as the man approached—*Hello. Hot, huh?*—and moved in front of Riley so that Riley couldn't see the man at all. *My my, it's something else,* the man said pleasantly. He looked like he might want to stay and talk, but his mother turned her back to him and leaned down toward Riley and said loudly—*Now, how are you, dear? Do you need a drink of water?*

She did not move until the man was well past, then she straightened up. Listen, Riley, she said, just don't talk at all, do you hear me? I don't want you to say even one more word, understand? I don't care what or who you want. Your father is not here!

She pushed on ahead. Riley hoped and prayed she knew where the Baskin-Robbins was. He didn't know where anything was, of course. And the sky suddenly got dark like it was going to rain, which made him think of hurricanes.

Mom, did you know that Mr. Loflin says this is the hurricane season? Riley asked, completely forgetting that he'd been forbidden to open his mouth.

Hush! Can't you hurry up? she said in reply. She squeezed his hand hard. They started down an alley.

Mom, why are we going this way?

It's the quickest.

The sun came back out from behind its cloud. Someone's trash can was full to overflowing and it smelled bad, like old fish. A window opened and shut somewhere—the sound made his mother's voice jump out of her mouth.

She was going to be a mess by the time they got to Baskin-Robbins if she kept on like this and he was probably going to faint, especially if they kept going down alleys that stunk so bad where there were no trees.

—Did you know that when the hurricanes come—he started up again to get her attention—they have to take all the kids out of the hospital and go somewhere because during the hurricane the ocean jumps over the Seawall. It jumps up over the Seawall even though it's made of—what's the Seawall made of? Mom?!

I have no idea, she said.

Are you sure? Riley said. Well, the ocean jumps the Seawall waves bigger than houses bigger even than the hospital it jumps the Seawall and comes rushing down through all the streets of Galveston—is this the right way to the Baskin-Robbins?

We're not going to Baskin-Robbins.

But I want ice cream! he cried in protest. The words just jumped right out of him.

She gave him such a look then, he knew she had no intention whatsoever of going to Baskin-Robbins. His heart sunk with disappointment, but he kept it to himself, just followed as she dragged him from one hot, sunlit alley to another.

Even so, the hurricane story had got ahold of him and he couldn't stop. He loved to think about hurricanes. They sent chills down his spine.

—And then the hurricane comes up toward the hospital the waves hitting and banging and crushing everything they touch and then even if they have a surgery going on even if the doctors are doing a graft on someone's face or even if all the big boys are down in the playroom playing pool everybody just has to stop whatever it is they're doing and get in the helicopters which are waiting on the roof or they'll be killed by the hurricane which is coming faster and faster every second—

36

Then finally they were in front of a tall, white house—*Here is Mrs. Griswald's boardinghouse*, she said—and she was fussing at him to hurry up the stairs to her apartment on the third floor and to keep his voice down so he wouldn't bother Mrs. Griswald.

—I think that they would have to have at least ten helicopters—he whispered as he went up the steps—don't you because there are four of us in our room and two over across the nurse's station then there's that girl from Tupelo they brought in last week though she's in really bad shape and might not make it I think that's all though I'll have to ask the tub men tomorrow if there are others and then there's all those kids over on the Reconstruction Ward except I don't know exactly how many kids one helicopter can hold—

She unlocked the door of her apartment and let him in. It was a nice place, Riley could see right away—full of windows in all the most extraordinary places and so cool after that long walk in the heat. There was a big room with a double bed in the center—it was easy for him to sit on because it was close to the floor, just the mattress and box springs. Right next to the top of the bed on either side were two little windows.

His mother sank down right away on the end of the bed. She took her fancy new sandals off and fell back, her legs sprawled on the floor and the rest of her flung across the bed. In a minute, she rolled over and pulled herself up and was sound asleep.

Riley was glad. He could poke around without her bothering him and he could finish his story without having to deal with her not listening, which she almost never did, especially lately.

—they would have to have something besides helicopters something bigger like an airplane—

First he went to her kitchen. He climbed up on the built-in seat by the kitchen table to look out the street-side window. But he could barely see the sidewalk so far below because of the tree branches. He could almost touch them. It was just like being in a tree house—a tree house with rooms and doors and windows and a kitchen.

Riley sat down at the kitchen table. She had books and stuff there, pens and pencils, and that big yellow notebook with her name written on it in big black letters—the one his father had brought that weekend when she was so upset. He opened it—she'd been writing inside on the lined paper in her fancy handwriting. Cursive! He couldn't read it any better than Melvin Pitts could. On the edges of the handwriting were little shaky pictures she had drawn in pencil of someone with a big head and big, fat lips that looked like one of the kids at the hospital.

He found an empty page and tested all her pens. He took the one he liked the best and drew a picture of two dinosaurs engaged in a violent battle. Fire shot out of their mouths and tiny men died with their feet in the air all around them. Above that skirmish, he drew a picture of himself in a shining red suit and blue cape surrounded by a glowing light. He would show his mother when she woke up.

Mom, he would tell her, this is how I've been all along.

You all along, my Riley dear? she would say. If I'd only understood.

Hadn't he told her a million times?

Nice. He shut her notebook and got up and went over past the refrigerator to the back door with the glass window at the top, standing on tiptoe to look down into Mrs. Griswald's garden. Oh, my—things were growing everywhere. There were poles that had signs on top of them, and stones and seashells at the ends of rows, and walkways all around and in between. Beyond the garden was a small house, and a lady on the front porch was talking to another lady—a big old lady—who stood at the bottom of the steps.

He stayed at the window a long time, cataloging everything he saw and trying to make out what the women were talking about while he drew to the whispered end of his hurricane story. —Where is Melvin? The helicopter is here and no one can find Melvin and here comes the hurricane all the trees are twisted up the waves are pounding on the beach OHHHhhh Melvin where are you there he is downstairs in the basement hiding in the closet come on out of there Melvin would you—

He walked back to her bedroom. With his knee on her pillow for balance, he leaned over to look out one of the odd little windows near the top of her bed. The pressure of his weight on the bed made her groan and roll over, her dress coming up above her knee. He pushed it back down and resumed his exploring.

At the other end of her bedroom was a bathroom, big, with a tub on four fat legs that was very deep—almost as deep as the tub in the tub room at the hospital. And a mirror! None of the bathrooms at the hospital had a mirror. He suddenly felt hot and uncomfortable.

Mom! Mom! he whispered in her sleeping ear.

Huh?

Mom, can you pull my mask off? She rose up, her eyes still shut, and felt around the back of his head for the Velcro opening on the brown hood, then pulled it apart and up and off his face. The white mask underneath, which Roland the mask guy had made from plastic he had put on Riley's own face, tumbled down onto the bed. It lay there while she fell back asleep and Riley went to look in the mirror.

HIS FACE SURPRISED HIM at first, took him off guard, shocked his system the same way Eddie's face had when he first saw it. He *did* look like Eddie, just like Melvin Pitts had said. He had to look down for a minute—just like with Eddie—then slowly back up at the mirror at least ten times before he could take it in. *Hmm, hmmm*, he said over and over, until it all began to come clear for him.

Yes.

He'd been thinking about a disguise for a long time. He'd felt it in his long, gangly limbs, this urging to be gone!—out of himself, someone other than Riley Martin. He was tired of being that boy who was always in everybody's way, who everybody said was so big.

—*Oh my, what a biiiig boy! He's such a baaaby for such a big boy!* Riley whispered to himself.

He hated the sound of it. Now he was tougher than nails—he could see it—like a dinosaur, like G.I. Joe, like the Bionic Man—plastered all over with layers of shiny skin. He would show them.

He admired himself around from all sides—his eyes were drawn down, his lips were swollen, no hair except for little, odd patches here and there, no ears, something about his nose, not there, just like the aliens on Star Trek—not a trace of the old Riley. That boy was gone, like he was dead, just disappeared off the face of the earth never to be heard from again—and good riddance. No one at all would recognize this new boy. He could be just whoever he pleased. He could scare the living daylights out of all the kids he met—especially those big sixth-graders on his block—and they wouldn't for a minute—for even a minute—know what he was thinking, because his new face hid everything. It was like a mask—stiff and hard. He was safe behind it. He could order his mother around with it if he felt like it. He tried making it move in the mirror, raising his eyebrows. But he had no eyebrows! He could barely smile or frown his skin was so tight. Good! Only his pulsing eyes showed his displeasure.

—All right now all of you, he said, marching boldly out through his mother's bedroom and round and round the kitchen, get a move on it do you hear me we're heading out of this hospital on the double this is an evacuation the hurricane is coming and I'm here to save all of you if you miss the helicopter just jump on my back and we'll fly right into the eye of the hurricane we'll blow it to kingdom come—

37

His mother sat up. Riley? Riley! What are you doing?

I'm ready to go, he declared.

Ready to go where? she said sleepily. We've only been here a half hour. I'm exhausted.

I want to see the ocean, he said, standing up tall and looking at her fiercely, trying out *the look* in his eyes—his new face would make her do whatever he wanted. I want to get an ice cream at Baskin-Robbins. I want a hamburger with fries at Rusty's. I want to go to the ocean.

Hold your horses, young man, said his mother. There's no way we can get to any of those things this afternoon, not walking—not even if we were in a car. She stood up in a wobbly sort of way. This heat will kill us before we ever even hit the door. It almost already has.

No, we're staying put, she determined, and slid back down on the bed.

Riley began to cry.

Listen to you, his mother said. You're acting just like a baby. Stop now! Go color something. There's paper on the kitchen table.

Riley sucked in a deep, shuddering breath. Tears leaked out of his eyes. That's not what Dr. Walker and Marilyn Hooper and the social worker told you to do, Mom! He stamped his foot. They told you to take me out to the Baskin-Robbins. Weren't you listening? I heard them! There's nothing to do here. You don't even have a TV!

There was a knock on the door.

Good Lord, now look what you've done, his mother said. She sat up, fully awake. It's Mrs. Griswald!

Riley heard her at the door. Yoo hoo, everything all right?

His mother grabbed him by the shoulders. Don't say anything! And stay right here—don't move!

She went to the apartment door and opened it. *Why, we're fine, thanks ever so much*, Riley could hear his mother say in the voice she used to talk to everyone else except him. *Just getting ourselves used to things. Riley's tired right now, you can imagine, he's resting, we'll come visit you some other time*, she went on.

Riley couldn't resist taking a peek. He liked the sound

of Mrs. Griswald's voice, a nice drawly voice sort of like the voices of some of the nurses at the hospital. He poked his head out just a little.

Well, there's the young man, Mrs. Griswald said suddenly.

Riley's mother turned and the look on her face was very dark.

How you, fella? Mrs. Griswald kept on. Come to keep your mother company? Riley inched along the hallway. Mrs. Griswald suddenly sucked in her breath. *Bless his heart*, she said, and her mouth dropped open.

Well, she said, catching herself, we've been waiting so long for you to come on home. Riley came closer to her. He figured his mother couldn't do anything much to him with Mrs. Griswald there. He liked her voice but he couldn't really keep up with what she was talking about. He looked up at her from time to time—she was very tall—but it hurt his neck to do it too much, so he mostly just stared at the floor.

A lot of folks had lived at her boardinghouse over the years, she was saying, and she was telling all about them and how they had grown up and come back to visit and were doing good despite all the tragic things that happened to them, which she began to list out. His mind drifted up and down with the sound of her voice.

Why, there was even a boy who'd lost his nose, Riley heard her say. He turned his face up now, wanting to know more about the boy who'd lost his nose. Maybe it was Eddie. He could feel his mother tense up.

Mrs. Griswald must have felt it, too, for she shifted the conversation suddenly, addressing Riley directly. Why, how old are you? You're such a big boy. You must be going into fifth grade, are you?

Second, Riley said.

My my. You *are* big! Well, if you're just going to hang around here, why don't you come on downstairs and have some pie with me and Arnold. He'll show you some of the junk he bought at the flea market this morning.

Okay, Riley said quickly. He would love to take a look at Arnold's junk and he would love to have a piece of Mrs. Griswald's pie.

Pie? No, thank you, he heard his mother say. We're just leaving to go do a little sight-seeing, aren't we, Riley? She glared at him. *Didn't we say we were going to Baskin-Robbins, dear?*

His heart sank. He'd wanted to meet Arnold so much. Sitting in Mrs. Griswald's kitchen seemed to him to be a really good idea. It would be cool there, they'd be inside, and maybe Mrs. Griswald would have some ice cream to go with the pie—that would be as good as

Baskin-Robbins any day. He wanted to say all these things, to point out how this invitation from Mrs. Griswald would solve all their problems—his mother's and his both—but he could see from his mother's face that she had no intention whatsoever of going to eat anything in Mrs. Griswald's kitchen.

RILEY AND HIS MOTHER left the apartment shortly after Mrs. Griswald clumped back down the stairs. Riley wanted to know why they couldn't just go eat pie with Mrs. Griswald and Arnold, but all she said while she was putting his mask back on was, *Bless his heart, bless his heart.*

They set out, turning right onto Church Street, heading away from the hospital. His mother tugged him by the shoulder of his shirt, one way and then another. That first block, overshadowed by towering dark trees, was quiet, as empty as a tomb, but on the second block there was a man rocking in a chair on his front porch. As soon as his mother spotted him, they shifted to the alley that was oceanside of Church, a place full of metal cans and noisy flies, broken seashells, and old tires. For the life of him, Riley couldn't figure out why she'd turned down that alley. It was just dirt and smells and heat—when it was hot enough already—and there wasn't a living, breathing soul anywhere to be seen along its entire length.

Are we on our way to Baskin-Robbins? Riley wanted to know. After all, Baskin-Robbins had been her excuse to keep him away from Arnold and Mrs.Griswald's pie.

We're on our way, all right. She pushed him on the shoulder.

They went on, creeping up one street, and down one alley, circling upon themselves until Riley was sure they were completely lost. Keeping to the alleys had confused his mother, he felt certain. It was a bad plan because once they got back on the streets and sidewalks, they were in a different neighborhood—no longer big houses painted white and green with red flowers in pots all up and down the steps, but only run-down shacks, some boarded up, others covered with big black letters.

Where are we, Mom? Riley said. We're lost. Where's that Baskin-Robbins? I'm hot. This isn't any fun at all. I can't keep going on like this. I need to sit down. Do you know where we are, Mom?

I'll tell you where we are, his mother exploded. We are in the middle of nowhere is where we are. And do you just want to know exactly how we got here?

She didn't give him time to answer.

We got here because *you*! thought you were such a big

boy and because *you*! had to do exactly what you were told not to do and because *you*! decided that you would like to learn a little something about gasoline like you've been told not to do one hundred times before and because *you*!—she turned and glared at him—decided to play with matches. We are here, because *you*! decided to set yourself on fire! That's why we're here. For that reason and no other. You decided to ruin everything because *you*! wanted to do what *you*! wanted to do. Oh I could kill you, I tell you, there are days when I could just kill you.

She started to cry. Riley really felt like he was going to pass out.

Do you hear me, Riley? She pushed him in the middle of his back. We're here because *you*! had to have your own way, just like always.

Whooo-wee! Riley heard a voice soft and low on his right. Three tall black boys wearing no shirts at all stood together on the steps of an old gray house. Something gold glinted out on the chest of the tallest. It caught Riley's eye—and his mother's, too, apparently, because she stood there squinting—it looked like the boy had a gold ring coming out of the nipple on his chest.

Jesus! slipped out of his mother's lips. Riley looked up. The boy was wagging his tongue back and forth like a snake's, rubbing it against his teeth, and he winked at

Riley's mother while the others boys hummed with laughter.

She pushed him across the street but there were men sitting on the porch of a house there, wearing very short cutoffs with their legs propped up against the banister—Riley could see right up their pants—and they were staring at him and at his mother. Then there was an old woman out sweeping the dirt in front of her house who stopped when Riley and his mother passed by. What happened to your boy? she said point-blank, but his mother didn't answer and marched right on past. They crossed the street again, heading down an alley but didn't get far—toward the end of it there was a bunch of men leaning against a car, drinking beer. His mother turned around quickly, but not before the men spotted them and began to spread out, yelling and waving at them to come closer. A hot wind blew out of nowhere, his mother's hands out so quick to hold down the skirt of her dress.

The next alley ended temporarily in a school playground, but there were no kids.

Why don't you swing? said his mother, pointing to a jungle gym sitting in the middle of the dirt yard. Swing some. Go play.

But the metal swing set was much too hot for Riley to hold onto and his mother was just as hot as he was, so they went on.

38

They set out again, moving through the heat like swimmers navigating a dense swamp. It surrounded them, a solid, molten mass emanating up from the broken-seashell-covered paths, a nearly impenetrable wall. The neighborhoods through which they passed seemed even more unfamiliar than the ones they had gone through just before.

Where are we? his mother said. Why is it so dark and dreary? But no, not so dark and dreary exactly, because the sun is shining somewhere, I know it's here because I can feel its heat, I just can't see it. And I don't see a single soul, where has everyone gone, oh Riley, I think everyone has disappeared. I can't even hear the traffic. There's not a thing here, just this field that needs mowing and these old houses, full of broken cars. Oh what is going on? Am I going crazy?

I want to go home, Riley cried suddenly. It was clear to him that she had, in fact, gone crazy. I just want to go home, he wailed. I want to see Dad. I'm hot and now I'm tired and I can hardly breathe.

Just give me a minute, Riley. I need a minute to think. She started talking real fast, like a person talks when they're freezing cold and their lips are chattering or like he sometimes talked when he got out of surgery, just talking talking talking, so relieved to be alive and so much in need of telling everybody everything on his mind.

I must be dreaming, she went on. It must be the heat. It's so hot. It's this heat, this oppressive heat. It's heavy enough to undo a person, and I haven't eaten anything all day—I just remembered—and my feet are killing me—oh why did I ever buy these stupid sandals and now I'm just completely turned around. Where in God's name are we?

Riley couldn't figure out how they were ever going to get back to the hospital, especially since he had no idea where he was, and especially since she didn't seem to be making any sense at all.

He heard a sound, just a little sound at first, someone crying, a child somewhere crying. His mother moved her head all around. She must have heard it, too, because the child crying somewhere got closer and his voice got much louder.

Help me! Somebody help me!

What's that? his mother wanted to know. She pushed ahead, pulling him along until she could find where the noise was coming from and there on the corner near a stop sign and just beyond the field of grass was a tiny boy with blond, curly hair dressed in a little blue outfit with red pockets and he was screaming his head off. *I'm lost!*

Oh, Lord, said Riley's mother and she raced forward, leaving Riley to stand alone. She caught up to the boy and bent down on one knee so she could be face-to-face with him. What's the matter, dear? she said. I'm lost, the boy wailed. I'm lost. I can't find my mother. *Oh help me,* he screamed, louder and louder, *I'm lost.*

The lost boy kept right on screaming. Why you're such a sweet little thing, Riley heard his mother say. Your mother would never leave you. Don't cry. You poor thing. But the little baby cried on. Oh please stop, she said. We'll find your mother.

And then she fainted, and her skirt flew up nearly so you could see her underpants and Riley rushed forward to push her dress down and suddenly there were people standing in a circle all around her looking down at her and one of them was the lost boy's mother, come to rescue him. And everybody wanted to help and wanted to get her a cab, but she was too embarrassed and confused and said she was fine and Riley was fine—though Riley tried to say he wasn't. He knew he wasn't fine and he knew she wasn't fine but he also knew that his mother would rather die than admit it.

I think there's a place right up ahead where I can rest, she told anyone who asked.

WELL, SHE SAID, HER voice all dry and muffled, as they trudged along, I couldn't have explained this day to anybody in a million years, this whole thing, this walk, this wandering, just like we were in some place that only existed in another world, some antediluvian place—have you ever heard that word before, Riley—antediluvian?—a place before the Flood? Only it feels like we're in the middle of a flood. Oh God, we've got to get out of this heat.

Riley was mad at his mother. He was embarrassed that she had fainted and that her skirt had come up and that everyone could nearly see her underpants and he was mad at her because she had gone off to rescue some kid who didn't need rescuing when what she really needed to do was to get him back to the hospital.

You could have just told that little boy to go find his mother, he fussed at her. He didn't need your help—really he didn't, Mom. *His* mother was right there.

He walked out ahead of her.

—He was just a baby that little boy he didn't need to cry like that his mother was right next to him and here he was making all that racket just like a little baby what a little baby he was those kind of kids make me sick I see them all the time at the hospital.

39

The old church appeared out of nowhere, a gray stone building with green grass, sweet-smelling bushes, and a stooped-over man tending the yard with a rickety push mower. The front door was open. They walked up the steps. It was dark and cool inside, and Riley was glad. It wasn't Baskin-Robbins, but he didn't care anymore.

His mother sat down in the first pew she saw and slumped against red cushions, her feet propped up on a wooden bar below the seat. Riley heard her groan in relief.

He walked up the center aisle. The church was like a black-green ocean of colored light and deep shadow, with here and there a little pocket of especially cool air. Slowly but surely he made his way to the altar where he stood studying the cross and the open Bible that lay there. He thought again about Lazarus coming out of his cave—one of the gravecloths covering his face. Could he see? Did he still stinketh? Would his sisters then have wanted to hug him? Did he take a bath right away? Was he hungry? After all, it had been four days—he must have been starved. He probably had to run quick and go to the bathroom and what would he say to all those people staring at him—*I have to pee?—hurry!*

He was about to go up and touch the Bible, maybe turn some pages and see if he could read anything, find that story about Lazarus—maybe it wasn't in cursive—when he heard his mother clear her throat in the back of the church. He turned and began to lace his way back toward her, up one row and down the next, in and out of the pews, running his hand along the tops of the benches as he went along.

It was nice here, cool. He'd been so hot and tired. He felt sleepy. He stopped midway and looked back at his mother to see if she was still watching him, but her eyes were shut so he sat down in one of the pews and took a red book out of the rack in front of him and spread it open on his lap. He couldn't figure it out—though he tried hard—but, really, he was much too tired to concentrate. If his mother could sleep in church, so could he. He rested his head back against the pew and felt his body pulse and let himself drift far away.

• • •

He heard a shuffling noise then and opened his eyes a little. A man was moving very slowly up the row that Riley was sitting in. Riley watched him, much too tired to move. The man's head came first—it seemed to float out in front of his body—his enormous eyes, magnified by thick glasses, hanging onto Riley's eyes. He had a big, frozen smile on a big, bumpy, square face and he just kept coming toward Riley as if he was going to press that face of his up against Riley's mask or maybe walk right on inside and through him.

Instead, he sat down right next to Riley. His breathing was heavy and his breath smelled strong. Riley leaned in a little to get a whiff of him to see just how bad it was and then he saw the man's hands, big hands with puffy fingers.

The man asked Riley right away about the mask that he was wearing. His voice had a gravelly catch in it, as if he were just about to cry. Riley told him all about the fire and the hospital and the tub men and the doctors. The man asked Riley how the fire started and Riley told him proudly that he had started it himself. He asked Riley if the fire had scared him and then it was the man who brought up Sleeping Beauty, not Riley, and it was the man who said that the whole thing about Riley and *his* fire reminded him of *her* particular destiny—how nothing at all was going to stop her from being pricked by that needle just like Riley was going to be burned no matter what. It was the way things had been set from the beginning and its course was absolute and unyielding.

Riley took a deep breath and shuddered. What a relief to find someone who saw things the way he did, though he wished maybe the man had been a little different, maybe more like his father. He wished the man wouldn't sit so very close to him—his breath was so strong. He did seem to know a lot and he liked to talk as much as Riley liked to talk. His voice was nice, the way it seemed he was going to cry any minute, as if he absolutely understood everything—every thought and every feeling—that Riley was telling him. And that made up for how hard he was to look at.

The man wondered if everything was working out the way Riley thought it would. Riley told him all about Melvin Pitts, about how really bad Melvin Pitts had made him feel and how he felt he couldn't bring himself to be his friend even though he knew Melvin needed a friend in the same difficult way that *he* needed a friend and how much churning in his stomach that had caused and how much he had wished at one time that Parker MacGwyn would have wanted to be his friend, and then how he'd met Eddie and how he wasn't afraid of Melvin anymore and how things had changed completely since Parker left. And he told him how much he missed home and Lady Luck, except that Lady Luck was dead. And he told him about Greg.

The man knew exactly how Riley felt about Lady Luck—*there's nothing like a good dog*, he said. He knew how Riley felt about Greg, too, even down to that certain smell Riley loved about Greg that was part and parcel of Greg's house: the smell of peanut butter and hot chocolate, which seemed to be mashed and soured into their couches and rugs.

Greg is really a wonderful boy, said the man, his eyes seeming to swim behind those heavy glasses of his, as if just the thought of Greg made him want to cry. No, there aren't many better friends than Greg.

Riley leaned in closer, looking at the man's eyes to see if he was lying about knowing Greg.

What's your name? Riley asked.

The man blinked very slowly, two times in a row, and then smiled a great big smile. Riley had the idea that he was somehow supposed to figure out the man's name from that smile, but he didn't have a clue and he didn't want to ask again. Maybe this was the Andy that Jackson and Johnson sang about all the time, the one who walked with them and talked with them—

The man went on as if nothing had happened. You know, he said, crossing his leg and patting the top of his knee with the tip of one of his swollen fingers, the real treasure in Room 312 is Melvin. Yes, Melvin, he said, as if he knew right away what Riley was thinking. It's always that way—the ones you least suspect. And Carnell—yes, Melvin and Carnell are really two of the most marvelous boys.

Riley had two long thoughts that seemed to come together at the same time: one was that this man—whose name just might be Andy—probably had never met Carnell or Melvin, either one. The other thought was a picture: Riley could suddenly feel Carnell beside his bed, his fingers poking at Riley's arm to come play, his hot breath—almost like Lady Luck's—next to Riley's cheek, checking to see if Riley was awake. Riley saw himself roll over and pretend to be asleep.

Carnell and Melvin? he thought.

They weren't meant to be your friends, the man said. Greg is *your* friend. And of course, there's Eddie. Now Eddie is a boy after my own heart.

Riley put his chin on his hands and started thinking about Eddie, wondering if he would ever see him again and trying to remember if Eddie had actually said he would be his friend or if he had dreamed it and—if he had dreamed it—wondering how this Andy knew about the dream and about what Eddie had said in the dream and if maybe they were both in a dream right now—he tried to wake himself up to see—but the man interrupted him.

Can you give me a hand with something? he asked.

What about my mother? I can't go anywhere. Riley turned in his mother's direction.

She'll be fine, the man said. She's very tired, she'll sleep through the whole thing. It won't take so long anyway. And we're not going anywhere. He stood up.

They dug up two rows of pews. They turned the rich, dark-smelling dirt beneath over and over. It really didn't take long, like he said, though the man—Andy—had to stop and wipe his forehead with his handkerchief, which, Riley noted with a little bit of squeamishness, wasn't very clean. From out of his back pocket, Andy took a tiny brown paper bag that was folded in half. He opened it carefully—his splotchy hands shaking and the paper cracking and crinkling in a way that made Riley grit his teeth—and put it in front of Riley. Riley looked inside. The bag was full of little yellow things.

Seeds, Andy said. Get one.

Riley put his hand in the bag and took one out. It was cool to the touch. When he closed his hand around it, it shone through his fist. He could see all his bones. The seed was perfectly round.

Andy's finger made a hole straight down deep into the dirt. Put that seed in there, he told Riley. Then Andy filled the hole with dirt, so the light from the seed could barely be seen anymore. Then he smoothed everything over and put the pews back in place.

They sat down again. That didn't take long, said Andy, but he sat for a long while, breathing very hard in a whistling, wheezing sort of way. His face was wet.

That seed, Andy said finally—and he turned to look at Riley with those hard-driving, bulging eyes of his—if it grows at all—is going to produce the sweetest fruit.

Riley looked Andy over carefully. His face was all red and full of ridgy holes—he was really just a mess, hard to look at—and his nose looked like a big knot, like somebody had beaten him up bad. His ears were ragged and there was hair growing out of them. His hands had brown spots on them and for a minute Riley felt sick, like he did when he was near strawberry milk or the smell of it.

Really, though, Andy continued, it will be a miracle—with how fat some of these people are who sit in this pew—if it grows at all. Then, of course, I have no idea if any rain can get here inside this church, what with the roof and all. And a seed does need water and sun. It won't get any sun in this place.

Maybe we should have buried it somewhere else, Riley suggested.

Oh no, Andy said quickly. No, Riley, this is the spot. This is the very spot. But let me tell you this, when it first comes up, if it actually does come up, it will be just a stick in the ground. Whenever you look at it, you'll think it's dead and it will remind you of how you came to this church and the circumstances you came in, hot and beaten in a way—Andy's voice cracked for certain and his eyes swam with tears—and your mother who you love so much so tired and cross. When you look at that stick, you'll think that nothing will ever change. You'll want to tear it out. You'll think that planting that seed was the stupidest thing you ever did. You'll even think it was just something you dreamed.

40

Andy shut his eyes very tight and smiled the biggest smile, as if he'd just remembered something.

Say, Riley, did you meet Eddie's sisters yet?

They were playing pool with me.

Aren't they something? Andy asked. Two of the world's most sterling girls. They've really been sisters, in every sense of the word . . . Andy shut his eyes, lost in contemplating the sterling sisters.

Pat will be like a sister to you, Andy said. Riley stared at him. Pat! Andy didn't know Pat and how mean she was or how ugly. She was too mean to be anybody's sister. His stomach took a turn for the worse.

How can she be a sister to me? She's not coming to my house—ever!

No, Riley, she's not coming to your house, said Andy. She won't be able to come to your house—ever. She's very sick.

Is she going to die?

Some people's hate is so pure, it's just like love. But it makes it hard to keep going.

Riley inched in a little toward Andy so he could look at him closer. *How the heck did he know anything about Pat?* Andy was smiling away, just thinking about her. Even Andy's smile was ugly, it was so big and so foolish. His face glistened with sweat. He scratched his head and then opened his eyes. What were we talking about, Riley?

About Pat.

Yes, what a girl! And what else?

That seed and the stick.

Oh yes! Andy clapped his hands together. Riley! Just at the moment when you think that you dreamed this whole thing up, he said triumphantly, the green leaves will appear. Oh, Riley, when you see those leaves, your heart—and Andy folded his hand over his own heart and let his head fall—your heart will nearly burst. And then the blossoms will come. They'll be white and creamy soft. And then! The fruit, yellow and orange, round and soft in your hands, and the first taste of it will be so—sweet. So very sweet.

Like peaches, Riley said

Ahh, peaches are very nice, but this will be better than

peaches, said Andy. Wait until you taste it! Oh, Riley, the fruit will come. It will come. But the waiting might very nearly kill you. Andy shook his head back and forth with excitement and Riley couldn't tell if he was going to laugh or cry. Andy put his face right up next to Riley's ear. If that seed grows, he whispered, it will be completely beyond what a *normal* boy can do. Do you understand?

Riley looked up at Andy. Now Andy was really talking. Riley thought with pleasure of his new face. Nobody back home will know who I am, he said. Except Greg. He'll know me.

That's right, said Andy. Nobody back home will know who you are. Except Greg.

I'll be like Superman, said Riley.

Oh yes, just like him. A boy nobody knows—moving around secretly inside yourself, attending to business only you know about. Your whole life will be hidden from view.

Hmmm, said Riley. *Hmm. Hmm.* That seed makes me think of Jack and the beanstalk, he said enthusiastically. He wiggled over a little next to Andy. That face of Andy's was almost like his smell: once you got used to it, you just wanted to get in closer. Really, Andy was the nicest guy. Riley could almost taste him. Delicious, like Greg.

Riley turned and stood with one knee up on the pew so he could get in close and study Andy's amazing eyes.

Riley? Andy said as they stared at each other.

Huh?

You cannot use your face to scare people. Or to bully them.

Riley sat back down. He was stung. In just the time it took to take a breath and with just that word from Andy, he saw his whole seven years laid out as neatly as the street he was raised on. He saw himself sitting so proud on the steps of his house—the big boy who had all the answers. He saw himself in his classroom waving his hand at every question the teacher asked. He remembered just how smart he thought he was when he decided to light that match. He saw his mother in her chair asleep beside his bed, her head back and her mouth wide open, the pajamas she had sewn for his teddy bear on her lap, and his father drifting alone in their house with Lady Luck dead in the backyard. Every word he'd used to mock Melvin and every word he'd used to push Carnell aside and every word he'd withheld from Pat whose heart—he suddenly saw—was dying for kindness, came back to him. Sleeping Beauty and Superman and Treasure Island suddenly lost all their charms for him. What foolish years he'd already spent—wasted. He felt pressed down, wishing with all his heart that the fire had never happened. He longed to go back to when he was first born, to a time before the fire. He wanted to start over. He wanted every single thing he did and said to be . . . clean.

He would never light a match again.

Andy's warm hand on his shoulder brought him back.

Do you have X-ray vision, Andy? Riley asked after a while.

I do see your insides.

Hmmm, hmm, hmm, Riley hummed. Then Andy knew *everything*. Riley sighed. He sat back up on his knees right next to Andy. He cupped his hands lightly around Andy's neck, pressing them slowly in and then out around Andy's leathery skin—he didn't even know Andy very well but it seemed like the most natural thing in the world to be inspecting him so carefully. Then he put his cheek against Andy's cheek and breathed deep, entering fully into everything about him—his smell, his difficult face, his lumpy hands—and stayed like that a long while, not thinking of anything—though visions of conquering the world by terrifying people with his face and flying over tall buildings passed in and out of his mind. Andy was talking: *Pease porridge hot, pease por-*

ridge cold, pease porridge in the pot, nine days old. Riley whispered it along with him: *Some like it hot, some like it cold, some like it in the pot, nine days old.* They said it together over and over and on the rhythm created by that old nursery rhyme, Riley received and understood these things: that Andy *was* ugly, that he was uglier than any man had ever been and ever would be, including Eddie—and Riley himself. That it was okay about the fire. That if the seed grew it would be, against all odds, Andy's doing—water, sun, the whole business. That the fruit, though delicious, would be hard to eat.

Right then Riley agreed with all his heart to eat the fruit, no matter what.

Andy leaned his head against Riley's chest. Riley felt a great heat coming out of Andy's forehead. He could see Andy's hair and his scalp as close as if they were under a microscope. There looked to be three colors: black and gray and another color—red? Orange? Riley studied Andy's hair with great interest—it was standing on end—while Andy removed the skin from Riley's body—so quick—it was like a white bandage unwinding—like Lazarus!—and Riley saw himself—oh my!—such a frail thing—but so clean—his heart spun out—and then he didn't.

The fire, Andy said, has burned away everything and when Andy said the word *everything*, Riley suddenly remembered that picture from school he made his mother bring—the one he was so proud of because he'd sat up so tall and looked straight into the camera—the picture that had made Melvin Pitts so screaming mad—and he let go of it—the picture—it was not a something to hold on to anymore. And he let go of his face forever and gave it to Andy.

Thank you, Andy said. And if ever you get to worrying about what is happening to you, Riley, just give me a call.

MUCH LATER, AFTER HE and his mother finally got back to the hospital and he had taken off his new clothes and put on his pajamas and his mother had gone home—and hopefully put away her dress—and Riley was lying in bed with the covers pulled up to his chin, he had wondered how he was ever going to give Andy a call—he didn't have a phone number—or how that seed would ever grow underneath those pews with all those fat people sitting on them every Sunday—but that was Andy's problem, not his—or how he would ever see that seed again, the stick or the fruit, if it did grow, since it was there inside that church in Galveston and he was going home to El Paso.

But he only wondered those things for a minute just before he fell asleep, because otherwise it was exactly the sort of thing that made perfect sense.